T0267514

NO GOING BACK

NO GOING BACK

PATRICK FLORES-SCOTT

Christy Ottaviano Books

LITTLE, BROWN AND COMPANY
New York Boston

Christy Ottaviano Books
Hachette Book Group
1290 Avenue of the Americas, New York, NY 10104
Visit us at LBYR.com

First Edition: April 2024

Christy Ottaviano Books is an imprint of Little, Brown and Company. The Christy Ottaviano Books name and logo are trademarks of Hachette Book Group, Inc.

The publisher is not responsible for websites (or their content) that are not owned by the publisher.

Little, Brown and Company books may be purchased in bulk for business, educational, or promotional use. For information, please contact your local bookseller or the Hachette Book Group Special Markets Department at special.markets@hbgusa.com.

Library of Congress Cataloging-in-Publication Data
Names: Flores-Scott, Patrick, author.
Title: No going back / Patrick Flores-Scott.
Description: First edition. | New York : Little, Brown and Company, 2024. | Audience: Ages 14–18. | Summary: Told over the course of forty-eight hours, seventeen-year-old Tony heads back to his old life in Des Moines, Washington, after being released from a youth detention center, but toxic old relationships and unforeseen challenges make staying on the straight-and-narrow nearly impossible.
Identifiers: LCCN 2023022625 | ISBN 9780316407502 (hardcover) | ISBN 9780316407700 (ebook)
Subjects: CYAC: Interpersonal relations—Fiction. | Family life—Fiction. | Parole—Fiction. | Racially mixed people—Fiction. | LCGFT: Novels.
Classification: LCC PZ7.F33435 No 2024 | DDC [Fic]—dc23
LC record available at https://lccn.loc.gov/2023022625

ISBNs: 978-0-316-40750-2 (hardcover), 978-0-316-40770-0 (ebook)

Printed in the United States of America

LSC-C

Printing 1, 2024

In memory of Peg Phillips for bringing theater
to incarcerated kids at Echo Glen Children's Center.
And to all the kids who bravely stepped
onto the stage and gave it a try.

Dear Reader,

Have you ever been stuck in a situation where someone with power over your future is judging you?

They're shaking their head at you, tsk-tsking you, and you can just tell they're thinking, "I will never understand people like you. But I know your type well enough to know that you are up to no good."

If the person judging you is capable of thinking those two opposite ideas at the same time—and they're in control of your destiny—you are very likely screwed.

So what do you do?

My first instinct is to run. But the last time I found myself at the mercy of judgers, I was stuck in a high school conference room with family, my guidance counselor, the assistant principal, and my parole officer. There was nowhere to run, nowhere to hide.

So I closed my eyes, took a deep breath, and said, I know this looks really bad, but...

And I didn't stop talking until I'd told my whole honest-to-God true tale of the seventy-two hours after my release from Zephyr Woods Youth Detention Center—the good, the bad, the ugly...including the improbable and gripping encounter with the same stolen money that got me stuck in Zephyr in the first place.

In the conference room that morning, I prayed that my story—the story you will read in this book—would convince all the judgers that the situation wasn't nearly as bad as it looked and persuade one of them that there was no need to send me back.

As you read my story, you will judge me too. That's all right. It's human nature to judge. In judging me, however, please keep these words in mind: On our journey to growing and developing into the ideal whole persons we hope to become, we are all just stumbling forward in the dark, searching to find our way the very best we can.

With gratitude,
Antonio Echeverría Sullivan

FRIDAY

SATURDAY

SUNDAY

MONDAY

FRIDAY 9:30 AM

The soles of my shoes drumroll the floor. My fingers tap-tap the table. My face aches from too much grinning, because finally, *finally*, the buildup is over and I'm sitting pretty at a conference-room table in A Pod, about to say goodbye to this tiny prison in the forest.

Admin Pod is way nicer than the resident cottages. There's newish furniture and carpet, some fake flowers in a vase, big windows, some inspirational posters on the wall. But don't get me wrong, it is still Zephyr Woods Youth Detention Center. Still an institutional facility. Lysol smell. Beige walls. Zappy fluorescent lights. The nonstop muffled sounds of walkie-talkies. The metallic buzzing and clacking of doors locking and unlocking. Sobs from the clinic or angry screams from some terrified kid they're dragging in on their first day—a new one who hasn't given up the fight. Prison living—am I right?

Well, the reason I'm bouncing in my seat, not giving a flip about prison living, is because this is my reentry team meeting. That means I AM OUT OF HERE! I am finally leaving this depression factory that has caused me so much loneliness and anxiety.

I smile across the conference table at Mrs. Williams, my counselor, and Ms. Duncan, my English teacher. They've been my resource team since I got put in here. And now they are the core of my reentry team. They smile right back like they're so proud of me.

I turn away and point out the window at the forest, pretending I spot a bald eagle, while I swallow the lump in my throat and close my eyes to keep tears from coming.

Despite the big effort, a couple drop and slide down my cheek.

Mrs. Williams holds out the box of tissues. I yank one and think how far I've come since she and Ms. Duncan watched me rage in here like a freaking hurricane.

Truth be told, even before I came into this place I was a soda can full of built-up emotional pressure. Getting hauled into Zephyr just intensified it. The humiliation of handcuffs and shackles. The fear of prison kids and prison guards. The fear of life without my best friend, Maya. The fear of life without freedom. The realization that I would forever be a *convicted felon*.

It all shook me so hard, I could no longer contain the pressure. I erupted, and my darkness spewed over the land. I screamed. Sobbed. Begged for my mom. I kicked. Flailed. No one would have believed I was capable of that type of nuclear meltdown. I couldn't believe it either.

At Zephyr it was nothing new. They had the protocol down. Two beefy, bald guards. Snug wraparound jackets. Copious drugs. Independent reflection time in a padded room.

When I finally gave up the fight, Mrs. Williams and Ms. Duncan kicked into gear. I'm happy those two ladies are here to celebrate this moment with me. At the same time, I get a twinge in my gut thinking about the people who can't be here. Two of them, Charlie and Maureen—the volunteer Alcoholics Anonymous chairpersons—are at their day jobs.

I ended up in AA because, after speaking with people at Puget High School, the court determined I had an issue with alcohol. I knew the *I'm not an alcoholic, I just drank too much* argument wouldn't get me anywhere, so when they said I had to enroll in a sober-support class at Zephyr—in my case, AA meetings—I just nodded and kept my mouth shut.

In AA meetings, Charlie and Maureen dug into the twelve steps. We had to admit that we were powerless over alcohol. We were instructed to make a fearless moral inventory, and told we needed to embrace a higher power and to ask our chosen HP to remove our shortcomings.

To be honest, that woo-woo stuff wasn't for me. In fact, I was just about to tune Charlie and Maureen all the way out, when they started talking about steps eight and nine.

These two steps guide you in making things right with the people you hurt because of your dependence on getting drunk. Everyone wants to live their life as a responsible person. Well, being a responsible person means you have to deal with the consequences of your actions. And that means making things right with the people you hurt.

I still wasn't sure if I was an alcoholic. But I was fully aware that I had an accountability problem. I blamed others for my hurtful actions. In AA, I realized that in blaming others, I was letting those people define and control me.

I decided I was through playing the blame game. From now on I would take full accountability, full responsibility for what I'd done. I began the process by doing step eight. I made a list of the people I had hurt and wrote down my plan to make amends.

On to step nine. *Making amends.* In this step you tell the people you hurt that you are sorry. You say exactly what you did, while making zero excuses for your behavior. If you do make excuses or blame others, it will be so obvious that you are not holding yourself accountable for your actions, the person you are apologizing to will just roll their eyes because you don't even get it.

After the apology, you promise the person that you will do everything you can to make things right. You complete the act of making amends by living your life according to those words. And if you stick to that plan, you just might repair a relationship that you had broken.

My only problem? I couldn't make amends to the people I hurt until I got out of Zephyr. So I thought about which staff could help me earn my parole ASAP. And I did what they told me to do.

In class, Ms. Duncan told me my life mattered. My experiences and memories mattered. If I could write them down, I could think about where I came from and where I wanted to go. So I started writing my most powerful memories in poems. Poems that tell the story of a great childhood. Poems that explain how it all came crashing down, how I committed my crime, got arrested and locked up in Zephyr Woods.

In counseling, Mrs. Williams told me the dark thoughts stewing and bubbling inside me mattered. If I could get brave and speak them out loud, they could be examined. So I started spilling my guts.

Close your eyes, Mrs. Williams would say.

Inhale deep.

Exhale slow and long.

Repeat until you can look at the thought and ponder it.

What is this thought doing for you? Is it worth holding on to? Is it worth acting upon?

If it is worth acting upon, what course of action will do the least possible harm to yourself or others?

Soon, I began to notice my thoughts outside of counseling. I could stop and breathe through them before my head and hands got tingly and my breaths raced away. And before I reacted in a way I would later regret.

I did all that mental work. And I kept a journal of the actions and attitudes required to impress people enough to earn my parole. Stuff like this:

- When you encounter Zephyr drama, walk the other way fast.
- Every action you take is a CHOICE YOU MAKE. Choose wisely!
- When they ask for volunteers, be the first to raise your hand.
- Listen in class. Ask questions. Do your work. Improve your grades.
- When you need to, do your breathing—try for six deep breaths a minute, like Mrs. Williams

taught you. Slow your heart. Get calm. Consider
how you will respond to that stimulus you found
so aggravating.

- Practice that which you want to do well. (An
example of this one is, I found a quiet place to
practice the words I plan to say when I make
amends to the two people in my life I hurt the
worst when I committed the crime that got me
shipped away from them when they needed me
most—Carmen Echeverría, mom; and Maya
Jordan, lifelong best friend.)

The old Antonio would have rolled his eyes at any kid who
journaled crap like that. I would have called that kid a tool. Turns
out, the old Antonio was the tool, because all the focus and effort
led to so much personal growth that I earned my parole after a
year and a half. That's six extra months of living life as a free
person!

And it's the reason I'm not locked up in a sensory-deprivation
cottage eating a breakfast that tastes like Styrofoam with a bunch
of hormonal, depressed, sweaty, overmedicated juvenile offend-
ers. Instead, I'm sitting here with Mrs. Williams and Ms. Duncan,
staring at the conference-room door, awaiting the arrival of my
parole officer and my mom, and counting the minutes until I get
out and I can see Maya again.

When We Were a Team

Once upon a time, on a wet spring day in first grade,
my mom asked me to join her
at the Waterfront Farmers Market.
In matching raincoats and fingerless wool gloves,
we stood behind a table
and sold her coveted salmon-themed mugs.

Sockeyes, Cohos, Chinooks.

I'd wrap the mugs tight in paper and
hand them over to a delighted buyer
while she offered informational tidbits
about the life of our region's most sacred fish.

As each customer walked away,
she'd smile and hoot, ¡Otra venta!
She'd raise her palm high. Gimme five!
I'd jump up and give it, then pump a fist.

We did it!

. . .

In her studio, together on the stool,
she'd wrap her arms around me,
cup my bare hands in her clay-smeared hands,
then set the wheel to spinning,
singing me songs she learned as a kid back home.

A mi lechero no le gusta la leche—
¡Pero quiere que lo tome yo!

She'd sing and sing as we pushed and pressed that
cold, wet blob till I thought it was done.

¡Ya Mamá!

She'd scrape my creation off the wheel,
lift it high, and call it beautiful.

Then she'd set it to dry and fire up the kiln,
treating my mess like a work of art.

She saw me like a work of art.

I saw her like a work of art.

And that was the case for a long, long time.

When I First Started Waiting for Maya

Then summer after first grade came,
and Maya Jordan moved in next door.

My mom said I had to play with her.
I told my mom I'd hide from her.
I told my mom I hated Maya,
even though I didn't know her.

When she came over, Maya could see I was shy.
But this little freckled kid was sly.

>   *It's okay, she said. We don't have to play.*

Then Maya got to work, silently stacking and stuffing
pillows, chairs, sheets, blankets, till she'd built a sweet sofa castle.

Then she sat alone inside it, quietly snacking on pretzels and apple
while pleasantly humming a song.

That kid was happy as a clam.

I slid closer to the castle. Closer to that Maya.
And I slumped. Slouched. Whimpered. Moped.
Until Maya saw I was sad.

Want to join me? she asked.

I nodded yes and crawled inside, where we sat and snacked
until Maya said there was something in her backpack,
something special she'd brought just to show me.

She held up the pack.

Close your eyes, she said, and reach inside.

I reached in till my fingers felt a rocklike object.
I gripped and lifted it—for its size, it was light—
and when it appeared, I was holding the biggest shell.

At one time, Maya said, that was the home of a moon snail.
I found it at low tide at the beach with my mom.

Then Maya leaned in close to me and whispered in my ear.
She told me she knew a fact—an evil thing these moon snails do
when they manage to capture a scallop.

It's a secret, she said. Can you promise me you'll keep it?

I solemnly promised I would.

That's good, she said. But it's time for me to go.
Hold on to that shell. And I'll tell you the secret tomorrow.

Waiting for her at the window, holding that shell tight,
I tried so hard to be patient.
But I couldn't wait. I couldn't couldn't couldn't.
I just couldn't wait to see Maya!

FRIDAY `9:40 AM`

The door buzzes and clacks. Officer Brian Murdock marches into the Zephyr conference room. His blond hair freshly buzzed, Murdock gives a half smile and a half wave, like, *Let's get to it. I got parolees to chase down!*

Just two weeks ago, Murdock Zoomed with me and my reentry team to talk about my parole. In exchange for the state letting me out of Zephyr early and offering some support, I had to meet the following terms and conditions:

- I can't break any laws.
- I can't leave the state.
- I have to be reachable by phone. I have to contact Murdock every week and return his texts promptly, answer his calls, or return missed calls within an hour. I have to let him know if my phone number or address changes.

- I have to be present for in-person daily check-ins with Mrs. Lucrisia, my Puget High School counselor, and alert Officer Murdock if anything comes up and she and I can't meet.
- I have to obey Puget High School's attendance policies. I have to let the office know if I'm going to be tardy or absent, and I have to call Murdock to explain.
- Obviously, I can't consume alcohol or illegal drugs. I have to submit to monthly drug testing and show Murdock proof that I'm going to a sober-support meeting on a weekly basis.
- I have to keep to a curfew, from nine at night till six in the morning.
- I may not knowingly hang out with anyone who is on probation or parole.
- I have to be on time to my reentry meeting with Officer Murdock and Mrs. Lucrisia and others on the Puget resource team in the Puget High School counseling office, at 7:00 AM on the Monday immediately following my release.

As Murdock goes over each of these terms, he keeps saying that if I break any of them, I could get sent right back to Zephyr.

In my mind I'm like, *How could I possibly break any of these terms? They're so basic.* Check in with Mrs. Lucrisia? No prob. The sound of her voice is like a hug and a warm cup of cocoa, even when she's at the end of her rope, begging me to *please get your act together for your own sake, Antonio Sullivan!*

Keep in contact with Murdock? I'm no fool. I can send and respond to texts.

I skim the list. It all seems like a joke until the very last term.

Murdock reads it out loud. "You may not have contact with your father."

The words throw me back into my chair and I can't stop smiling, and inside I'm like, *Thank you, thank you!*

"Your dad has been made aware. Your mom knows too. You may not initiate contact. And if your father tries, you have to let me know immediately. Or else..."

I don't even consider the *or else*. Because knowing my chaos-agent dad can't be anywhere near me gives me the confidence to know I can go back home and live life right.

"Is that all clear?" Murdock asks.

I nod yes. Because it's awesome.

But then I feel it, a tug from way down deep. My body reacts to it before my brain can make sense of it. My breaths get short and fast. My hands pinprick-tingle. I squeeze them together, like I could stop this. But I got a feeling ball in my gut, and I know where that thing is headed. It travels up to my lungs. Then it's stuck in my throat. I swallow hard, but it shoots up and presses against the backs of my eyes. My shoulders shake.

There is no hiding it. The tears flow, and I'm about to bare-hand a bunch of snot and wipe it on the bottom of the table, but Mrs. Williams hands me a tissue.

And as I sit there wiping my face, I am so grateful for this term. Because even though staying away from my dad seems like the easiest thing in the world, I might need help dealing with that tiny part of me that says I'm not ready to let go of him. Not ready to let go of hope for us. Because letting go of my dad means letting go of who he used to be, who *we* used to be together, way back in the day.

When He Was a Hero

So then, when I was in second grade,
after months of my dad working so hard,
he sat at the edge of my bed and announced
the upcoming grand opening of . . .

"The Crypt!" . . .

his comics shop he'd built from the bottom up.

He thanked me for my patience, all those days I'd waited.
He smiled with appreciation and handed me a paper bag.

I slipped my hand inside, gently pinched, and slipped out . . .

Green Lantern, Martian Manhunter, Captain Marvel, Shazam!

My dad read me the comics one after the other.

Superheroes tossed aside random bad guys,
then ambled home alone, until . . .

The biggest, baddest, most evil villain rolled into the dark city,
their first stop in a master plan to conquer Earth,
the galaxy, the universe!

My superhero dad sprang to his feet!

Arms extended, he flew, swooping round and round until,
suddenly, he fell flat on his back, captured and
trapped in the villain's cruel killing machine—
a contraption designed with our hero's weakness in mind.

I stood up on my bed. I hopped up and down.

Go, Dad, go!

My dad was the best almost-die-er,
come-back-to-life-er, strength-regain-er,
villain-vanquishing save-the-day-er!

I cheered him on until, at last . . .
the villain was gone.
And the hero had won. Then . . .

Next comic! I'd beg.

Just one more, my dad would say.

Just one more, I'd say.

Just one more. Just one more. Just one more.

FRIDAY `9:45 AM`

Another *buzz* and *clack* and the door springs open. Carmen Echeverría glides into the room like there's wind in her sails. Her eyes are bright, her cheeks so full and red, and *that smile*. Her hair is cut short and sassy. She's sporting an artsy shawl and tall boots.

My mom is a new person! Or like her old self from way back before her health and her life went into the dumpster.

My mom last came to Zephyr a year ago. A few months earlier, just after I got locked up, she was prescribed a cancer drug that improved the mysterious autoimmune issue she'd been battling for years. Then she got pregnant. Sharing the baby's immune system seemed to help her even more. Even with her progress, doctors put her on bed rest for months leading up to the birth of my new sister. So she couldn't make another trip out to Zephyr. After Olivia was born, there was no way.

All that time, when we talked on the phone, she'd kept telling me she felt a lot better. I had no idea she'd be like *this*.

We make eye contact. Her smile stretches wide and she spreads her arms. I can't help but burst out of my chair and run across the room and hug my mom. And even though it couldn't ever take the place of a real talk-it-out step nine, our hug feels like she's saying stuff to me and I'm saying stuff to her and our pasts—the gnarly parts—are gone. Not *gone* gone, but like we're ready to say and do the stuff we need to say and do so we can move forward as mother and son.

"Antonio," she says, holding my cheeks in her hands, her eyes widening. "¿Estás listo?" Two words, and I know she's asking me if I'm ready for everything. To go home, to meet my sister, to meet her partner, Claudio, to live our best lives together.

"Listo para todo, Mamá," I say.

We get settled, and Mrs. Williams starts by talking about what needs to be in place for a successful transition to life outside Zephyr. The most important thing is me being the same Antonio she's seen this past year. She talks about the change she saw in counseling, how I made a shift toward taking full responsibility for my mistakes and for paving the way toward a new direction in life.

My mom squeezes my hand under the table every time she hears something positive.

Mrs. Williams talks about my strategies for dealing with obsessive thoughts and negative triggers. She turns to my mom, emphasizing phrases like *planning ahead* and *on the same page* and *open lines of communication* and *establishing trust*.

Ms. Duncan tells my mom I'm ready for Puget High School. She talks about my new study skills and discipline. She says that hard work led to my parole.

As the meeting winds down, I get light-headed and nervous. I grip my mom's hand tight.

Mrs. Williams gives her a packet of information on mental health and support services.

Officer Murdock goes over my conditions for parole. My mom isn't fazed when he reads the term about my dad. Murdock slides her his business card, and she adds him to her contacts.

My mom signs papers that say we did all the parts of the meeting and she's been made aware of the terms of my release and her and my responsibilities. She pushes the pen my way.

I breathe deep, sending out messages to all the people who helped make this moment possible. *I will not let you down.* I write in my best cursive. I cross the *t*, dot each *i*, and hand the paper and pen to Mrs. Williams.

"We're proud of Antonio," Mrs. Williams says.

My mom smiles huge at me. "I am too."

She and Ms. Duncan say the nicest goodbyes. So nice, I break a rule of Zephyr. I hug those two ladies.

They break the rule right back.

FRIDAY 10:40 AM

At the front desk, I sign a paper and hand it to Mrs. Neville. In exchange, she gives me the trash bag that followed me from juvie in Seattle all the way to Zephyr Woods. I dig inside until I find my phone and charger. I scan the waiting room for an outlet.

"Behind the bench," Mrs. Neville says.

I plug in and wait for a sign of life. I am sure there'll be texts from Maya waiting for me. Maya, who wondered what happened that day when I didn't come home. Maya, who found out I was locked up and who probably texted every day in the beginning, hoping I might see her messages. Maya, who probably even texted once in a while after realizing I didn't have access to my phone. She messaged me anyway. To feel connected. To the idea of me. Even if she couldn't connect to the real me.

The screen finally shows a charge. I power up and thumb the notifications. There are dozens of texts.

But none from Maya.

Which means that ever since I got sent away, there have been no visits, no letters responded to, no phone calls, and no messages from Maya, the person in my life other than my parents who I've known the longest and cared about the most.

When We Discovered Where
the Magic Was

In third grade, Maya's dad ran out on them,
taking their car and most of their money.
So then, when Maya's mom, Rhonda, was at work
or needed a break, Maya would come over and play.
It happened so much, she wasn't just a guest.
Our house was her house. And we had the best time together.

On her days off, Rhonda took us to the beach.
We'd ride the bus, hop out on Pac Highway,
and run down to the mud and sand and water.

We'd flip big rocks and little logs, and peer into puddles.

Rhonda would spot
limpets
anemones
periwinkles
and tell us all about their lives.

Maya and me would reach in the water for

sea stars
urchins
hermit crabs
squealing at our discoveries.

After snack, Rhonda would say, You two go and play.

In our rubber boots, we'd stomp puddles and pools.
We'd race away from tides. We'd walk and walk and walk.

I remember Maya telling me how things would be
when her dad came back.

I remember telling her I bet he'd come back soon.

And when we spotted a great blue heron,
a bald eagle,
a seal,
or on the rarest, most special occasion, an orca,
it was like witnessing magic, and we just had to make a wish.

Every time I watched Maya close her eyes and make her wish,
I closed mine and wished there'd be more days just like this.

There are no texts from Maya.

But a whole string of them from that Gary Jr.

My stomach turns at the thought of him. My breaths get short. My hands get tingly.

A voice inside reminds me, *That's a feeling, Antonio. It's connected to a thought your brain created. You're letting that thought get the best of you.*

Close your eyes and breathe in deep.

I breathe in deep.

Exhale slow.

I exhale slow. And I pocket my phone. And say goodbye to Gary Jr. forever.

My mom bounces my way, smiling like a kid at Christmas. "We can go, right?"

We turn to Mrs. Neville. Her stone-cold grimace melts into a warm, hopeful smile. "Antonio Sullivan," she says, "you are free to leave." She beeps the door lock, and I hear the last Zephyr *buzz* and *clack* of my life.

But before I even take a step, she says my name again, her smile replaced by a withering glare. "I do not—I repeat, *DO NOT*—want to see you walking back through that door ever again. You hear me, young man?"

"I'm not coming back, Mrs. Neville. *Ever.*"

My mom hooks her arm around mine. "¡Vamos, Antonio!"

We march toward that door. She pushes through. I stop. Her arm slides out from mine. She asks me if I'm all right.

I lean my back on the door, sunlight warming my face. I deep-breathe that fresh Olympic Peninsula air till I'm all fueled up. I scan the parked cars. I gaze up at the towering evergreens. There is no fence between me and them. No fence between me and home. No fence between me and Maya.

I make this moment a choice. I'm gonna leave whatever is left of the old me right here. And take my next step as the new person I am.

When my foot lands officially outside Zephyr, I pump a fist in the air.

Just then a huge maroon Ford pickup passes us. It's Officer Murdock, flashing a smile and a peace sign. We watch him go.

My mom points to an old green Subaru she got since I went away. I drop my bag in the trunk and turn back to that prison in the forest for one long, last look.

Goodbye, Zephyr Woods Youth Detention Center, you asshole!

I barely get buckled and my mom is already in reverse. She shifts into drive, then silently lifts her eyes to the sky. "Mira, Antonio," she says, pointing.

A great blue heron glides just above us. Its sliver of a pointed beak, the kink in its neck, those wing feathers lined up, each one pointing out, its stick legs trailing behind. I can't help but think it's a message sent from Maya. *Come home, Antonio.*

I close my eyes and send a mind message right back.

And I make a wish.

FRIDAY `11:37 AM`

Headed south on Washington's Highway 101, passing tiny Olympic Peninsula towns. Eldon. Lilliwaup. Potlatch. Endless evergreens and the rocky barnacle beaches of Hood Canal.

I roll down my window, inhaling salt and the rotting fish-mud-seaweed mix of low tide aromas. Even though we live on the other side of Puget Sound, it smells like home.

My mom is smiling. Her skin is glowing. She looks so strong. Like back when she used to haul sacks of clay like they were nothing. Like my mom before stuff got in the way. I want to get past that stuff. For good. I need her to hear the words that start the journey toward making amends. I need to do step nine.

Can I do it now? While she's driving? Should I wait till we're settled in the house?

I need to do it where I can focus. Where she can really listen. We planned on lunch in Tacoma. I'll do it then.

I look over as her eyebrows scrunch. Lips tighten. Cheek twitches. What is she thinking?

The car slows. She pulls into a little park overlooking the water. "Venga, mijo." She gets out of the car. Arms wrapped around her midsection, she walks toward the only picnic table.

I undo my seat belt. Pop the lock. Reach for the handle. Lean against the door. And I freeze as my breath comes in fast. Goes out fast. Too fast. I haven't opened a door in forever. It's like I need permission, or like I'm afraid of what might happen if I do.

She turns to the car and waves for me to come.

Inhale deep, Antonio.

I inhale deep.

Exhale slow. I close my eyes and breathe like that until I'm in control and I can finally open up and walk out into the cool spring sunshine. The canal is a dark, beautiful blue. There's a rusty fishing boat stranded onshore. A trawler pulls away from its dock. A yellow catamaran skims the water.

She takes a seat on a bench. "Siéntate," she says, her hair blowing in the breeze.

I sit.

Her chin quivers. Her shoulders scrunch.

"What's going on, Mamá?"

She brushes hair from her face. Wipes the corners of her eyes. "I *left* you, mijo."

"No, Mamá, don't do this. You don't have to—"

She raises a hand to quiet me. "I do."

"You weren't getting better. And he was getting worse."

She wipes her cheeks. "I left you. If I hadn't—"

"You never would have met Claudio. I wouldn't have a sister. Dad would still be dad. You would probably still be sick."

She looks at me like I'm not wrong.

I tell her I was old enough to know better. "*I* did what I did. *I* made my choices. That's not on you or anybody else. It's on me."

"I just need you to know—living at Tammy's—me dolía vivir aparte de vos. Cada día, cada hora, me dio tanta pena. Not having you close. Knowing I left you with him. Knowing what he's capable of. I am sorry, mijo. I'm so sorry."

"I get it, Mamá. But that's over now. You don't have to feel like—"

"I feel what I feel." She grips my shoulder. Stares into my eyes. "Estoy contenta. Por fin tengo toda mi familia. I'm healthy, mijo. Almost my old self again." She stops and gazes out at the water. "Antonio, no matter what happens, I promise I will never be the person I was when things got their worst. I won't let anything get in the way of being the best mother I can to you."

I nod at all that.

"Forgive me?" she says.

"No," I say. "There's nothing to forgive."

"Nothing?"

"Nada."

"¿Estás seguro?"

"You did what you had to do," I say. "It was the right thing for us. Because here we are."

She wipes her eyes with a tissue. Rests her head on my shoulder. We sit quiet like that in the cold, salty air.

"Tammy was hard on you," she says.

"Next topic," I say, because that lady is not my fave.

"She's my best friend, but when you'd visit, she treated you like—"

"It's okay, Mamá. She was taking care of you. Protecting you."

"She was. The best she could."

"How's she doing?"

"Good. She pops in and checks up on me all the time."

Sitting side by side like this. Looking east across the canal. The Cascade Mountains looming green and brown in the distance. Somewhere between here and those mountains is my new life—our new life—together. But before we get there, it's time for step nine.

"Mom?"

"Yes?"

"There's something I have to say."

"Okay, mijo. I'm listening."

"It's just…"

"What, Antonio?"

"This is really nice." That's all I say. Because doing step nine right now would come off like my apology was a response to hers. Step nine is not about responding to the other person, or getting caught up in what they did or didn't do in the past. It's about *me*, and holding myself accountable for the damage *I've* done. It's about keeping *my side* of the street clean.

"It is nice," she says, reaching out for a hug. "It's a beautiful day. Now let's get home."

In the car we decide to skip lunch. This is the longest she's been away from Olivia. I'm good with it. I cannot wait to meet my sister.

When the Sofa Became Her Home

So then . . . one day in fifth grade,
my mom came home from work,
complaining of pain and exhaustion
that just wouldn't go away.

She collapsed onto the sofa.
And, soon enough, she just wouldn't get up.

No more shaping clay in her studio.
No more reading me long chapters at bedtime.
No more nights with my dad in their room.

Just TV and sleep on the sofa.

A series of question-marked diagnoses followed.
Chronic fatigue? Thyroid disease? Fibromyalgia?
Lupus? MS? They never knew what it was.

Tissue boxes and blankets on the sofa.
Bottles of water, bottles of tea, on the sofa.

Bottles of kombucha, bottles of pills, on the sofa.
An injection kit, and so many shots, all administered on the sofa.

My dad stepped up, managing like a champ,
while struggling to hold on to his comics shop.
Doctor visits, hospital stays,
hospital bills, prescription bills.
Scraping to pay rent and utilities,
making my lunches, signing the slips.
Seeing me off to school.
And setting my mom up every day,
with everything she needed, on the sofa.

We arch over the rainbow span of the Tacoma Narrows Bridge, then make our way onto I-5 north. Next stop, home!

I plug in my charger. I have to let Maya know I'm on my way home. Immediately, those Gary Jr. texts stare me in the face. I'm going to delete them all, until I notice the date on the last one. It's from two days ago.

> You out yet? Let me know! We have to finish this thing!

This thing was finished the day Gary and his idiot buddy, Vaughn, ratted me out. I delete the message. There's another one from a week ago.

> Ran into ur "dad" he sed ur getting out?!?!
> He asked ?s about what happened
> after the robbery. I didn't say one word about
> the $. Waiting for you my bro! So hit me up
> A-sap!

Ps: he looks really good.

Pss: why is his drug dealing ass not in prison?

I'm never going to see either of them again. Nothing Gary has to say about my dad or the robbery or the past matters. I hit delete.

There are a bunch more texts from when I got thrown into juvie, just as Gary Jr. got released. Stuff about some deal between our lawyers.

This deal did not turn out like my lawyer sed. I m sorry Tonio! So so so so so so so so so so SORRY!!!!!!!!!!!!!! 😭😟😭😟

I am ur friend. U r my friend. Look in ur heart! I m praying to you look in your HEART and believe me how sorry I am. I AM THIS SORRY:

SORRY!! !!

But sorry is a word, and a word can't make it right. Action can make it right. You and me are going to take action. And we are going to make it right.

I have no idea what he's talking about. Whatever it is, it's part of my old life. Gary Jr. is too. I have turned the page. And I'm not looking back. With a text, I make a clean break from Gary Jr.

I don't care. Do not text me. Do not call me.
Ever. Bye forever. FOREVER.

Then again, there is no way Gary Jr. wouldn't return that message. I don't hit send. I delete it and erase him out of my contacts. Out of my life. I won't text him. I won't ever tell him goodbye face-to-face. But I can take in a deep breath.

And exhale Gary Jr. out of my life for good.

My mom reaches over and touches my cheek. "¿Todo bien?"

"Yeah," I say. "Todo está perfecto."

FRIDAY `1:05 PM`

We exit off I-5 and wait for the light to change on Pac Highway and Kent–Des Moines Road. To the north, across all six lanes, in front of the 7-Eleven, a sign reads WELCOME TO DES MOINES, WASHINGTON.

Everywhere, I see ghosts of me and Maya crisscrossing these wide lanes of highway at all hours. There's the orange Westernco Donut sign atop the brown corner building. We spent so many late nights in that place, getting full on doughnuts for cheap. There's La Plaza shopping center, where we'd grab a loaf of day-old Wonder Bread at the market before heading to Saltwater State Park.

My mom drives past those ghosts and into the heart of Des Moines.

The pull to Maya is so strong, I have to see her as soon as I possibly can.

> I'm out. I'm home. I miss you. Quick walk around the block tonight?

When We Chose to Go It Alone

It was the summer after sixth grade...
My mom so sick on the sofa,
it was too much to keep track of me.

My dad, fending off calls from bill collectors,
running to the Crypt and back,
checking in on my mom,
checking in with doctors,
administering shots, taking her temp,
counting out meds.
It was too much to keep track of me.

I got lost in the shuffle, became invisible.
Left to fend for myself in a home that
kept getting darker and more depressing
with less and less stuff in the cupboards.

All I wanted to do was run.

Maya knew it. Plus—between her mom's boyfriends
and the stresses from struggles with money—
she had reasons to run too.

So then... a knock on the door.

I opened up.

It was Maya, in her swimsuit, hoodie,
and bright-red movie-star shades,
looking California on that grayest day.

> *What are you waiting for? she asked.*

Then, in the singsong Uruguayan Spanish she'd
picked up from years of listening to my mom...

> *¡Cerrá y vamos, bo!*

We ran away fast, winding our way south and west,
all the way down to Marine View Drive,
forty-five minutes, then a right into Saltwater State Park.

Stomachs growling, we reached into Maya's backpack,
pulled out our food, and set it on a blanket.

I spread mustard on Wonder Bread for her.
She spread mustard on Wonder Bread for me.
And we stacked bologna slices high.
Stuffing napkins in our collars,
lifting those sandwiches, with pinkies extended,
taking polite bites, calling the meal "delightful,"
calling each other "dahling,"
gorging like royalty in court.

First time I've ever been here, Maya said,
without my mom.

Maya looked at our crumbs,
a sad smile lighting up her face.

This is when she would say,
You two go and play.

We gathered our supplies:
a tiny net, plastic bucket, and magnifying glass.
We waded, backs bent, eyes on the water,
capturing and examining the teeniest, tiniest creatures.

Get close, Maya said, pointing.
Can you see those little swimmers?
Those are plankton.
There's phytoplankton in there too,
but it's too small to see.

Plankton eat the phytoplankton.
Krill eat the plankton.
Salmon eat the krill.
Orcas eat the salmon.

So there would be no orca families living in our sound—
no J Pod, no K Pod, nor L Pod—
if it wasn't for the tiniest, microscopic-ist...phytoplankton!

Everyone worries about the whales.
Focus on the plight of the phytoplankton!

Interesting, I said, nodding my head.
I had never thought about that.

Stick with me, Maya said, and keep your eyes on the water.
There's a lot more to learn where that one came from.

So close to grungy Pac Highway, so close to messed-up home,
but Saltwater State Park was far away enough.

Cuz on that rocky beach, the view is water, sailboats,
ferries, snow-packed mountains, evergreen islands, and Maya,
her black curls dancing in the wind, freckles darker by the day,
looking famous in those shades, keeping me alive with the
best sandwiches I ever ate, teaching me to dig deeper,
and to think about things I couldn't even see.

North on Pac Highway, left on 222nd, right on 24th. We finally turn into the driveway of a tiny house with a fresh coat of blue paint. The lawn is a deep green, neatly trimmed along the edges.

She steps on the brake. Pulls out the key. Smiles at me. "Here we go."

I unlatch the seat belt. Squeeze the door handle. I inhale a big deep breath.

And let it out long and slow.

I push open the door, step out, and squint in the sunlight. I grab my bag and watch my mom walk to the front door.

Claudio opens up. He's got my sister in his arms. He's dad-rocking from side to side, beaming at my mom. Claudio's not tall. But he's thick. Sturdy. He's sporting black science-nerd glasses and a goatee.

My mom kisses Olivia first. Then him.

"Antonio!" Claudio says, waving me over. "We meet at last." He shifts Olivia to one arm, reaching a hand out to shake. "How are you?"

I tell him I'm good and it's nice to finally meet him.

He holds Olivia up for me to get a good look. "Your sister has been dying to meet you."

My heart pounding, I get another lump in my throat and the feeling that this day is too perfect. Cuz Claudio is lowering my baby sister into my arms.

Whoa. I was not expecting her to be this heavy. Or this light. She's got my mom's nose. *My nose!* My mom's black hair. She's so perfect. A whole person in my arms. Her little breath. In and out. I'm holding her whole life.

In my head I'm like, *I am not going to drop you. I am not going to let anyone hurt you ever. I am not going to let you down. What games will you like? I can't wait to play them with you. What will your favorite color be? Your favorite cereal? I can't wait to watch you become the person you are meant to be. I'm going to do whatever I can to help you make it happen.*

I turn to my mom and Claudio. "Nice work, you two." Then back to Olivia. She puckers her lips and closes her eyes, her whole face scrunching.... *CHOO!* She shivers.

We all laugh at that big tiny-baby sneeze, and it feels like a good time to hand her over. My mom takes Olivia in her arms and heads indoors. "This is the living," she says, gesturing to the room.

First thing I notice is the sofa. Nothing on it but decorative pillows. No blankets. No throw-up bucket. No pillbox or injection kit. A wood lounge chair with a bright-colored cushion faces the sofa. There's a comfy yellow recliner. A little flat-screen. Art books on a coffee table. The room is small, but she's decorated it thrift-store cool.

She takes me past the tiny kitchen and dining room with a little round table and four curvy green plastic chairs. There's a sliding door leading out to a patio and the yard.

Then it's down the short hall, past the bathroom, and left through a bedroom door. There are tagged clothes on the bed. Jeans. A winter jacket. T-shirts. A wool sweater. A hoodie.

"Wow," I say. "This is a lot."

"Try it all on. If there's anything you don't like..."

At Zephyr, they let us wear street clothes. Two pairs of jeans and five plain T-shirts. Wasn't much. But it was easy.

"We'll go shopping for the rest. I just wanted you to come home to some new stuff."

There's a little wood desk in the corner. "Is this mine to use?"

She smiles. "Seguro que sí. This is your room, mijo."

It makes sense I'd have my own room with stuff in it that's mine. It just never fully sank in that the place I was going to would be *my home*. I lived a couple years without my mom before Zephyr. And even though I was in the only house I'd ever known, it didn't feel like a home. It hadn't for a long time.

There are a few little framed pictures on the desk. I pick one up. It's Abuelo Hector and me on his last yearly visit from Uruguay. "I didn't remember pictures of just us."

"There are more," she says. "They're still in boxes."

In this one, my grandpa's got his chest all puffed out, his eyebrows scrunched, real serious. He has his arm around my shoulder. I'm holding a soccer ball, smiling like it's the best day of my life.

In the months he was here, my grandpa dropped me and Maya

44

off at third grade and picked us up when my dad was at the Crypt and my mom was working at the credit union. When Maya went home, he'd take me to the park and we'd replay historic Uruguayan World Cup goals. He would call out the year, stadium, opponent, score, time left in the match. Then he'd get me in the right spot and tell me which foot to kick with—depending on how the goal had been scored. Finally, he'd pass the ball. I'd kick it in and he'd do the announcing. *¡Gooooooooool! ¡Alcides Ghiggia termina a Brasil con una gran patada! ¡Viva La Celeste! ¡Viva Uuuu-ruuu-guay!* He'd lift me up. I'd thrust my fists in the air, like a Uruguayan soccer god.

When he gave me my Diego Forlán jersey, he told me Diego was right-footed but worked so hard, he turned his left into a cannon too. So he could shoot at any time from anywhere on the field regardless of what the defense was doing. It was his power and flexibility that made him great.

For some reason, the jersey was an adult large. It fit like a dress on me. Didn't matter. Wearing it made me feel like I was a part of the team from the smallest country ever to win a World Cup, a team that uses brains, toughness, and grit to slay giants.

My abuela Ángela died when my mom was a little girl. My grandpa dying a year after his last visit hit my mom real hard. And him and me in that picture.... It shakes me up even now.

"He loved Diego Forlán," I say.

My mom smiles at that. "Before he came, he called and told me he'd bought you a Luis Suárez jersey. I told him I didn't want my son associated with a dirty player who bit an opponent in the World Cup. He said I'd been away from Uruguay for too long.

45

I told him I'd never let you wear it. So he showed up with his second-choice jersey."

I ask her if she knows where it is.

"Mijo, your dad has some of our things still. I'll ask him. It's going to take time, though."

I'm okay with it taking time but pissed off at the thought of him having our stuff.

Claudio pops his head into the room. "I wasn't sure if you'd eaten. Dinner won't be ready for a while. You up for a sandwich?"

My mom takes Olivia to her room to feed her and put her down for a nap. I follow Claudio to the kitchen.

When the Seams Burst

So then, in seventh grade,
my dad came home from the Crypt.
I hid and watched from the kitchen,
because too many years of
burning too many candles at both ends
meant my dad's calming down with one drink
had become drink after drink just to cope.
And now it seemed like so long ago
that he turned himself from a kind, warm person
into a person we didn't know.

He stumbled in and plopped on the end of the sofa,
glaring at my mom as she snored and slept there,
then slurring loud words about how much she'd hurt him.

My mom woke up. She said she needed her shot.

    My God, Carmen! he erupted.
    Do you ever think about me?
    If it wasn't for you, I could—

She summoned her strength, sat up, and said,

Don't blame me, Bradley!
This is what those vows mean.

After so many years of appreciating his sacrifices,
she'd grown tired of his reminders
that he had to make them because of her.

Sometimes marriage isn't pretty, she said.
But it's not my sickness that makes ours ugly.
It's you.

My dad pulled his arm back and slapped her.

She laughed in his face.
Then, glaring, she slowly rotated her head
and turned the other cheek, daring him.
And with a withering stare, she told him she was over him,
her heart closed to him, she'd never give in to him,
and someday she'd win.

She would.

But until that day came, he made it as hard on her,
as hard on me, as hard on us, as he possibly could.

Claudio hands me a ham sandwich off a cutting board.

"Bring it with you," he says, "I wanna show you something."

I take a big bite of that sandwich. "My God," I say, "I've been on a steady diet of laboratory-produced food replacement for a year and a half. I'm not used to food *tasting*."

Claudio laughs and tells me it's ham with jack cheese on home-made wheat bread, with homemade mayo and pickles he canned himself. If I only eat Claudio's ham sandwiches for the rest of my life, I'll consider myself lucky.

We walk out the patio door toward an old shed. He punches a code into the door handle. "It's 0526. Your mom's birthday."

I think, *Why's he giving me the lock code?* Then I'm like, *Why wouldn't he?*

I step inside and my breath is taken away. There's a pottery wheel. A little kiln. Real wood shelves—not junky particle board—up and down the walls on all sides. The whole place smells like that wood. It's not fancy. But it's exactly what my mom would want.

I turn to Claudio. "You did all this?"

"Yeah," he says. "I been doing part-time handyman work and driving Uber ever since I lost my union gig, so I have a flexible schedule. Figured I'd make myself useful."

My mom told me Claudio had been an electrician for the school district until he was laid off a few months ago.

"I hauled out all the junk. Polished and sealed the concrete floor. Sealed the exterior. Rewired the whole thing. Put in insulation. Drywall. Ventilation. When we met, your mom told me about her old studio. I knew that, first chance I had, I was gonna get her set up again."

"What does she think?"

"She thought I was just cleaning out the shed. When I showed her, she started crying, saying how much she loved it. But it's been a few months and she's never used it." He chuckles and shrugs his shoulders. He's not upset. Just curious.

"She's busy with Olivia," I say.

"Yeah," he says. "And maybe something else?"

I don't say it. But I'm pretty sure I know.

"There's something I want to make clear," he says, motioning from him to me. "This is *our* house. Your mom's. Olivia's. Mine. *Yours*. No need to ask to grab food out of the fridge. No need to ask to come out here or to watch TV or crash on the sofa. Do whatever. Feel free." He repeats himself. "This is your house."

I smile at him. "Message received."

"And I want you to know that nothing that happened before this moment matters to me. We all have our junk." He scratches the back of his head. "I sure as hell have mine. But that stuff isn't who I am now. You've got your junk. But that junk isn't who you are. You and me . . . we're just two people trying our best."

FRIDAY `8:20 PM`

After an unsuccessful attempt at an afternoon nap...after counting and recounting the hours till my Monday meeting...after non-stop checking my phone for a reply from Maya...after a dinner of Claudio's chile stew and homemade tortillas made with love and lard just like his abuelita's in Sonora back in the day...after the tale of how he and my mom met squeezing avocados at Albertsons... after I kiss my sister's chubby cheek good night...after taking my first steaming-hot shower since I first got put in juvie...

I slip into bed and am squeezed tight by heavy, tucked covers. Warm in my new cozy sweats, head floating on a feathery pillow, I yawn a huge one. I ball up. I stretch out. Ball up and stretch out a bunch of times till I find my sweet spot. My body sinks into the mattress...and I'm actually going to sleep. I'll wake up tomorrow with forty-eight hours to go till my meeting. And I'll kill those hours right here in this house.

I'll find the perfect time to do step nine with my mom. I'll play peekaboo with my sister. I'll read to her. I'll watch TV. I'll go nowhere. Do nothing until I leave this house for my Monday meeting and my first day of school.

Nowhere, that is, except a quick run to see Maya after she texts me back. I just need to check in. To make sure she's okay. To see her eyes. Her curls. Her freckles. To hear her voice. To hear what she's up to with school and life and if she's still dreaming about becoming a marine biologist. Then finally, after all this time, I'll do step nine and she'll see just how much I'm taking responsibility for my actions and for my life, and we'll start getting back to being us. But not the old us. A new, deeper, healthy us.

One more massive yawn.

Then a knock at my door.

"Antonio?"

It's my mom. Forget tomorrow. I'm going to do it right now. My heart pounds as she flips on the light and walks right at me. I sit up and tell her we need to talk, but she says it at the exact same time.

"You go first," I say.

She takes a seat on the edge of the bed. "I am so impressed by you. How hard you worked. How far you've come. And I couldn't be happier you're home."

"Me too."

She clears her throat. "Antonio, you're a young man now."

Okay, weird.

"But, until you turn eighteen, and while we work through this transition, I am responsible for you. Just know that all I want is for you to have everything you need to be happy. I wasn't the mother you needed for so long—"

"I told you, you don't need to—"

"So it's hard for me to talk about rules."

"Huh?"

"Tenemos que hablar sobre las reglas."

"Rules? Sure. Not a big deal."

"The judge and your parole officer said no drinking. You can't break laws, of course. And you have to have good attendance."

I get a knot in my stomach cuz I can hear it coming.

"You see how that's all connected, right?"

I squeeze the bedcovers in my fists.

"It's *Maya*," she says.

"You can trust me now." It comes out like I'm begging.

"I think I can. I think I can trust Maya too. But let's hold off a little while."

"She's my best friend," I say.

"I don't want to lose you, Antonio."

"There's no way I would do anything stupid."

She sits up taller, her jaw tightening. "I'm being the parent I promised you I'd be. You may not see Maya. Not until we're sure that you—"

"That I what?"

"That we are feeling solid. With school. With your AA. With this whole parole thing. And with our communication—no secrets, right?"

I ask her how long it might take for us to feel solid.

"We'll feel it," she says. "We'll know."

"Days? Weeks? Months?"

She sees it on my face. Hears it in my voice.

Tears roll down her cheek. "Revisit in a few weeks?"

Oh my God, I don't want this. But I don't want her to cry. Cuz none of this is her fault. It's my fault. I'm the one who made mistakes.

I reach my arms out. She wraps her arms around me. I squeeze. She squeezes.

I swallow hard to stop tears. "I'll wait to see Maya."

"Ay, mijo," she says, like, *That was hard, but we did it.* Then she says, "That Gary kid too. Okay?"

"No worries," I say, "I never want to see his face again."

A cry from the other room. She points toward the door. Stands and tucks my covers. Pulls them up to my chin. She runs her hand through my hair. Kisses my forehead and walks out.

In a second, she's walking back into the room with Olivia. She stoops so I can kiss my sister's cheek one more time. I don't think I've ever really smelled a baby. I get a pretty good whiff and finally understand what the fuss is about.

"Buenas noches, hermanita," I say. "Que duermas con los angelitos."

My mom hits the lights as she walks out.

I close my eyes and burrow into my covers.

This is fine. It really is.

You and Maya can text.

You can talk on the phone. You are lucky to be in this house.

Be grateful. Be patient. Be good.

When We Held Hands, the Sand Came Alive

So then...fall of eighth grade,
out of the blue, Maya's dad showed up.

Despite their tempestuous past, her mom took him back.

Maya seemed happy. Until a week later,
a sobbing afternoon call.

     Antonio, she said, he hasn't changed one bit.

I ran next door, stopping at that crack in the sidewalk,
gazing up at her window, waiting.

Maya burst out the door. She wore a winter coat
and a stuffed backpack, and she ran at me,
reaching out her hand.

I reached out, grabbed ahold,
and held it tight in mine.

And we ran as thunder rumbled,
the sky opened up, and the rain beat down.
We ran and ran, Maya and me, holding hands.

We ran all the way to the pier,
then jumped the rail and scrambled underneath.
The smell of tarred pier planks above us,
we scurried up the back beach to the driftwood pile
stacked high by years of winter storm tides.

Maya reached into her backpack.
She took out a blue tarp and a fleece Seahawks blanket.
We wrapped ourselves up,
our backs against the pile of logs and limbs.

We had just held hands as we ran from the storm.
Would we again?

We gripped the tarp and blanket,
and pulled them up to our chins to keep warm and dry.

Then Maya's closest hand let go.
It slid to my hand and rested on my fist.

I flipped my hand over. Her palm dropped into mine.
Her fingers slipped between my fingers.
She squeezed. I squeezed. We sighed.

You're nice, she said. Stay that way.

I will, I said, knowing how easy it'd be to stay nice to Maya.

Wondering why it seemed so hard for her dad.

And wondering about my dad—
if it was life that took his kindness away,
or if his kindness had all been a lie.

When the rain stopped, we packed up
and walked to where mud and rock ended.
Strolling, holding hands, thrilling at the neon-green explosions
that flared with our steps in the sand.

Bioluminescence, Maya said.
Tiny organisms lighting up like fireflies.
People look at sand and see only sand.
Huh-uh, she said, the beach is alive.

The whole way home, I thought about the way
people had begun to look at me.
I could tell they saw an empty, lifeless kid.
But Maya showed me they were wrong.
Cuz the neon-green explosions reflected in her eyes that night. . . .
Nope, they said, Antonio is alive.

Bzzt!

My eyelids pop open. *Where am I?* I sit up. Just enough light to see the desk. I'm at my mom's! I check the clock. I've barely been asleep.

Bzzt!

My phone! I grab it and check the message.

> Che vos! Ur out! ¡Bárbaro! Who r u staying with?

It's Maya!

> I'm with my mom. She's doing a lot better.
> What about you? I can't believe it's you Maya!
> How r u???

I can't believe it's you Antonio Sullivan! I'm doing all right. On solid ground. Thanks for asking.

That's so great to hear! That's really so great!

I've come a long way.

I don't *want* to leave the house. Seriously. I am all about staying put. But it's right there in my parole terms. I have to do AA. And step nine is AA. And with Maya, it's gotta be in person. So if I don't go do step nine with Maya, that means I'm violating my terms. Emotionally, *and legally*, seeing Maya is a hump I have to get over, a bridge I have to cross.

Mrs. Williams's voice pops into my head. *You're working really hard to justify, Antonio. Why do you feel the need? Let's dig into that.*

I shake my head and tell Mrs. Williams her services are no longer needed, then make a silent promise that after tonight with Maya, I won't break curfew again. I won't sneak out with her or even ask to see her until we all feel like I'm solidly on track.

I have something important I need to say. But it has to be in person. Nice night for a walk. Meet in front of your house? Like old times?

We do need to talk. Not tonight, tho. Not sure when. I'll text you.

I know that's hard. It's hard for me too. But it's for the best. Abrazotes hasta que nos vemos. Take care of yourself, Antonio Sullivan. Good night.

Good night?

Good night?

I throw the covers back and spring out of bed, feet on the floor. Feet moving.

Bed to the door.

Door to the desk.

Desk to the door.

Door to the window. I can't stop pacing. Because the way me and Maya are—the way we were—neither of us ever shut down an opportunity to get outside for a walk together. Around the block. Around the whole city. Down to the pier. Sometimes those walks lasted all night.

Now she's like, *I don't know when? Sometime? I'll let you know?* What she's really saying is, *Whatever we had is over. We are over.*

Breathe, Antonio.

I can't!

Bzzt!

You know who you should reach out to? Gary Jr. ASAP

When Maya and Me Met a Dreamer

So then . . . spring of eighth grade,
we were looking to keep cool on a hot May day.
So me and Maya crawled toward our
driftwood spot in the mud and shade.

But before we got there, we heard a whistle-chirp.
We looked to see where it came from,
and back in our spot, tucked in the shadows,
knees to his chest, sat a dirty blond kid in a stained pink polo.

There's space for two more! he said. Come on over, guys!

He pleaded to us with the most pathetic puppy-dog eyes.

We turned to scoot to make our getaway,
but the kid stood up and shouted,

Stay. Please, please stay!

Maya couldn't say no to those dopey eyes.
So we sat, and the kid started talking.

His name was Gary Jr., a ninth grader at Highline High.
He loved dirt bikes. He loved movies.
Watching them. Talking about them. Making them on his iPhone.

And as much as he loved movies, Gary Jr. loved weed!
And he pleaded for us to smoke with him.

> *Come on, guys! Please?*

Cuz he was missing his big brother, Stevie,
the person in this world he looked up to and dreamed with,
the person he used to smoke the most with.

Stevie had just dropped out of Highline College
and run off and joined the navy.
Now Gary Jr. was stuck home alone with his
super-Christian parents, who were nonstop on his case.

> *THEY THINK I talk too woo-woo about stuff that's not God.*
> *THEY THINK me making movies on my phone is stupid.*
> *AND THEY are threatening to ship me off to boot-camp school*
>   *in the desert.*

That threat fired up Gary's runaway anxiety, so . . .

> *Please, he begged, please, please, please,*
> *can't we all just smoke together?*

We told him we wouldn't, cuz we're not into drugs,
but we'd be fine if he did.

Gary Jr. sighed. He pulled out a baggie,
laid out the papers and the stuff,
then rolled the blunt, showing us
that when it came to weed,
Gary could be still, silent, steady, settled.

He lit up, sucked in, held on, exhaled,
then talked and talked our ears off,
going on and on about his fave cult classics—
Eraserhead, Gummo, Scanners, Blue Velvet—
twisted flicks we never even heard of.

Pointing his phone at me and Maya,
Gary directed us to gaze at the water.

    I knew it! he shouted. The camera adores you!

Then he begged us to act in his first feature.

    I guarantee you will love this film, he said.
    It's gonna be super Jarmusch.

Jar-moosh? We didn't have a clue. Didn't matter.
We felt his passion, creativity, drive.
The kid was on a quest for life's deeper meaning.
And the way his eyes lit up as he talked,
he made us feel like he'd discovered a bit of it in us.

I switch to all caps.

> I SHOULD SEE GARY JR??? R U
> F-ING KIDDING ME MAYA!?!

> I am not.

> Have you been seeing him?

> We talk. He's a good listener. I been through
> a lot since you went away. GJ helped me work
> stuff out.

> GJ!?! "GJ"???? Does he have a
> cute new
> nickname for you too????

And he is a good listener? Are we even talking about the same GARY??? 😂😂😂🤣🤣🤣🤣

Just see him. He has a lot he needs to say to you.

U understand what he did to me, right?

Yes! That's why you need to talk to him. Gotta run. Take care, you.

I throw my phone. Collapse on the mattress. I press my fists into my chest as my heart tries to ram its way out of my body.

I cannot stop the pounding. I cannot stop my breath. I cannot stop images.

Gary drooling, all gaga, as he listens to Maya talk about her problems.

Maya smiling back at him, a twinkle in her eye. Cuz his listening skills are so developed.

The two of them flying kites. Licking ice-cream cones. Exchanging valentines.

I start crying and wiping snot, worried my mom and Claudio are going to hear me. But I can't stop blubbering because of Maya and Gary on a Ferris wheel stuffing cotton candy in each other's mouths.

A buzz! Another text from Maya!

I grab my phone. It's not Maya.

> Tonioooooo!!!!!!!! Maya sez ur back
> Finly!!!!!!!!! Where u @ my bro???

I want to poke a finger in his stupid face. Describe the sick details of my life ever since he turned on me and got me sent to prison. Then punch his nose into his brain and tell him to stay the *f* away from Maya.

Breathe, Antonio, Breathe.

Mrs. Williams is right. I gotta breathe and get calm. I will do that. But first I have to put an end to this.

> GO TO HELL, "GJ"!!!

> Lol!!! U ARE THE THE BEST!

> Serious I hate u

> I know u do. But it still hurts bad 2 read those words sed 2 me by u my dear old friend

> Im so sorry for every single thing I cosd us.
> I will try u later my bro I will not give up on us!

> Don't bro me. Don't text me.
> Don't call.
> This is it. WE ARE DONE.
> FOREVER.

I press the power button. The screen goes dark. No more Gary Jr. *Ever.*

No more Maya until she's ready.

No more phone tonight.

I check the clock. Do the math again. Fifty-seven hours to go until my meeting.

My eyelids get heavy. I yawn. I stretch. Despite it all, I feel sleep coming. But before it does, I reach for my phone one more time. Murdock has to be able to reach me. It's a parole term. I can't disappear on him. I can't be AWOL.

I power right back up and block Gary's number.

I close my eyes one last time. Then...

Bzzt-bzzt! Bzzt-bzzt!

I just blocked Gary. And it's not Murdock's number either. I pick up anyway, worried it might be him.

"Tonio, don't hang up!"

"How the hell? I blocked you!"

"Pro tip: Hang on to that landline, my bro."

"Bye, Gary."

"It was the lawyers!" he wails. "The lawyers!"

"Sure. Right. Uh-huh."

"Let me explain!"

"No"

"Meet up."

"No."

"Doughnuts."

"No."

"Tonight."

"No. Not tonight. Or any other night. Got it? This is good-bye. We are over, Gary. No more you and me. Forever."

"I just need to see you! To explain to you! I need a shot. Just give me a shot! One shot!"

FRIDAY `10:52 PM`

I tiptoe down the hall. Press my ear against the door. My mom is snoring. Olivia must be sleeping. At dinner, Claudio told us he'd be out all night running people to the airport and to and from shows and parties in Seattle.

I pull on jeans. Slip into shoes. I stuff pillows under the covers. Put my backpack where my head should be. There's a clock radio on the desk. I find some white noise. Turn it down real quiet. But loud enough to sound like there's human activity in the room. Same routine from when I first started sneaking out with Maya— before the routine became meaningless.

I throw my leg over the windowsill and jump. I find a little twig and put it on the sill so when I slide the window, it doesn't shut all the way, and I won't accidentally lock myself out.

I move slowly away from the house, trying to keep in the shadows till I'm walking south on 24th. A few porch bulbs are all the light you get here. Black-green fir trees tower in front of and behind every little house. They cast their long shadows. A dog barks. A tomcat screeches. My heart races every time I'm lit up and blinded by headlights.

I used to love being out like this. But after so much time locked up at Zephyr, the world feels too big. I want to run straight back home and remake my bed till the covers are tight, then slide in and feel warm and safe and calm. Because I know seeing Gary Jr. is wrong. My mom says it's wrong. My parole terms say it's wrong.

But I need to stop my mind from spinning, to get answers to questions I can't stop asking. Why won't Maya see me? Why does she want me to see Gary Jr.? The kid cost me a year and a half of my life. Why is she fine with that?

I need to hear it from him. Then I need to punch his face. Cuz I can't move on until I do.

I stew like that the whole way down to Des Moines Memorial Drive, up 222nd until I'm finally out of the trees and darkness. Just a few hours ago, I was on my way home, coming at this spot from the opposite direction. Now I'm standing beside the WELCOME TO DES MOINES sign, staring across the intersection of Pac Highway and Kent–Des Moines Road at Westernco Donut.

If you stood here at rush hour, you could see hundreds of cars in one minute. People heading for the I-5 on-ramp on their way to Seattle or south to Tacoma. Or they're exiting off the ramp and headed home. This time of night, there's barely any traffic. I could cross anytime.

Doesn't matter. I can't get my feet moving. Cuz we shouldn't be meeting here. Gary Jr. is enough to deal with. Grace Cho, Westernco's owner, is a whole other complicated relationship.

Grace helped Maya and Gary and me celebrate birthdays at Westernco. She slipped us doughnuts when we were hungry and broke. She let us hang out as long as we wanted when it was rainy and we had nowhere else to go. We covered a couple shifts for Grace when she needed to run errands. She even gave me a job before I got sent away. Westernco is not just a doughnut shop. Grace Cho is not just a shop owner.

I head to the massive crosswalk. Traffic signals and walk lights flash. A jumbo jet flies low overhead. A lonely car zooms past. Across all these highway lanes, through Westernco's wall of windows, I spot Gary Jr. waiting alone at a table, lit up in fluorescent light.

My heart and breath race. My fists ball up.

Grace walks into view. She hands Gary a coffee and starts chatting.

In a minute, I'll be popping in there, pissed off, raging at Gary. That's not how I want Grace to see me after all this time. She deserves better.

She walks out of view, toward the counter. Gary stands and stretches big. Jumps up and down. Sits again. Then he gazes out the window, across lanes of Pac Highway.

I turn my back and walk fast because I did the math. Jealous rage + I want to crush GJ's face = nothing but trouble for Antonio.

Behind me, car horns blast, truck horns blare, tires screech.

I spin around to see cars swerving, drivers doing all they can to avoid Gary Jr., who is waving his arms and shouting at me as he Froggers across all six lanes. "Tonio!" he shouts, running right at me. "Tonio!"

I lift hands to my ears and shake my head like I can't hear.

Finally, he scrambles onto the sidewalk and stops, bent over, hands on knees, fighting to catch his breath, his middle finger in the air, saluting all cars. "Where were you going, Tonio? Grace fried up a batch of lemon-filled just for you."

"I came here to punch you. And you're not worth—"

"Punch me?" he says.

My jaw clenches. I glare at Gary Jr.

"Hell yeah!" he shouts. "Punch me! Do it! Punch me!" He walks at me, arms wide. "Everything you got. Right in my face, Tonio! Right in my nose! Pop it!"

"Stop it, Gary."

"Pop it, man! Pop it!"

Gary grabs my hand and tries to slap himself with it, but I pull away and walk. He follows me like a damn puppy. "Just drop in and say hi. She's selling Westernco."

I stop in my tracks. "Grace is selling?"

"Yup. We might never see her again."

"Damn." I walk faster.

He keeps right up. "Can you imagine if we counted up how much we owe her for all the doughnuts she slipped us over the years? At least say hello to Grace."

I keep walking.

"I can't have you hating me, Tonio! I owe you too much."

I pick up the pace until I'm running. Gary Jr. stays right at my side, begging me. I know he will follow me all the way home if I don't go eat a doughnut.

I stop. "Ten minutes, Gary. That's all you get."

"I need a solid twenty."

"I'll give you five."

"Give me ten, Tonio! That's all I'm asking."

"Ten minutes. Not one minute more."

FRIDAY

"It is so good to see you, Antonio." That's what Grace says, but her smile is forced and her eyes are asking twenty questions.

"It's good to see you too," I say.

"I assume that jail did not allow you to write letters, make phone calls, or email...."

"You good?" I say. "You and Tommy? The doughnuts? How is everyone?"

"How am I? I didn't go to jail. That's how I am."

My head drops.

"Chin up," Grace says. "You look at me."

I look at her.

"We took you in. Two weeks you were here every day. You slept in the back room. Baked doughnuts with Tommy. Worked the counter with me. We fed you good meals. You started look-ing healthy. Happy. You went back to school. Then—*pffft!*—you were gone. Not a word."

She points at Gary. "Then this one struts in and tells me he just got out of jail. And you got put in." She holds her hands to her chest like she's reliving the horror.

"Sorry I didn't reach out," I say. "Sorry I left all those shifts uncovered."

"Shifts? Is that what you think I care about? *Shifts?* I don't care about shifts! I care about your life!" She walks back to the counter. "You know, Tommy and I never could..."

We'd heard it a bunch of times. She and Tommy weren't able to have kids. They didn't have family around, so she said me and Maya and Gary Jr.—*the Outsiders*, she called us—were as close to grandkids as she was ever going to get.

Grace works hard at a smile. "It's okay. Really. I'm just happy you're back." She grabs her phone and bounces our way, motioning for us to get close. She hands the phone to Gary Jr. and tells him, "Selfie-stick us."

When we're done with the photo, Grace says Tommy's heart can't handle the long hours or the doughnuts. "We bought a condo on the Big Island," she says.

"There's volcanoes in Hawaii," I say.

"There are volcanoes here," she says.

"I know, but those volcanoes have molten lava."

"And these?" she says. "A lahar off Rainier would cover everything from mountains to sound in twenty feet of mud and ash. When that happens, I'll be sitting pretty in the sunshine on my balcony slurping saimin and sipping okolehao."

"I would like to visit you," Gary says, "and make a documentary about your life."

"Do it. Come to Hawaii. You too, Antonio. Bring Maya

with you. Sit back, relax, roll camera, and I will tell you my epic tale."

Gary's expression says he wishes we were the kind of people who could fly off to Hawaii to make a movie. He stares out the front window. "What's going to happen to this place?"

Grace points south. "You know RecMeds down Pac Highway?"

Gary Jr. turns to me and mimes lighting up.

"They want to buy the building and the business. They're going to sell pot, pipes, edibles—their gummies are to die for—the whole line of CBD. And they want to sell Westernco doughnuts. Doughnuts and weed. That's one-stop shopping."

Gary huffs in disgust. As much as he loves weed, he hates that news. I do too.

Grace pokes my shoulder. "Where you staying?"

"My mom's." I tell her how good my mom is doing. And about Claudio and my sister.

"Oh, Antonio." Grace puts her hand to her heart again, but this time with a big sigh of relief. "That is so good to hear." She points to the booth. "The Outsiders came to talk. So talk." Grace walks behind the counter and folds takeout boxes. But she keeps her eyes focused on us.

I slide my butt into the orange vinyl booth, taking the spot behind the glazed lemon-filled resting on a napkin. Gary sits across from me, his maple bar untouched. He won't eat till I do. He's polite like that.

I take a bite, and *damn*, Tommy's lemon-filled crunches the tiniest bit through the glaze and crust. Then it's a cloud of dough on the inside. Then—*zing!*—that tart hit of lemon.

As I chew, I check the place out. My eyes land on a fading Seafair poster hanging on the fake-wood-paneled wall. It's got the schedule of where the pirates will be each night. Maya used to look at it and say, *Arg! Seafair, nineteen ninety-seven!*

A string hangs down from a yellowing plastic fluorescent light fixture. I swear it's left from a few years ago when Maya hung balloons in here for Gary Jr.'s birthday. His parents were off at a Foursquare Church convention, so she threw him a party. She invited a ton of people, but not enough came. She asked Grace if the homeless guys hanging outside the Westernco could join us. Grace knew them all by name, so she said sure. We sang to Gary, and then Grace talked those guys' ears off. After it was over, she made sure they all left with bags of doughnuts.

Gary Jr. snaps his fingers in my face. "Are you here with me, Tonio?"

"Yeah." I pull out my phone and set the timer. "Ten minutes. Then I'm gone. And you may not follow me home."

Gary's head pokes out of a too-big puffy jacket. His lip starts trembling. Then his whole body. His face scrunches as he tries to hold tears in, but some drip onto his maple bar.

"That's not gonna work, Gary."

He exhales long and loud, then chews on a bite of the bar. He burps into his fist and says, "I need you to listen, Tonio. And I need you to *hear*."

"You have nine minutes."

"So I'm in juvie a few days, right? I'm waiting for court stuff to happen. I get called in to see my lawyer. He sits me down and tells me the DA says if I agree with what Vaughn already told them, I can get off with time served."

"What did you tell him?"

"I didn't tell him you planned the robbery."

"Who told them?"

"Idiot Vaughn! He told them him and me did the robbery but you were the mastermind. You decided on the date and time. You copied the house and safe keys. You made a map of the place. You told us about the alarm system. Vaughn spills all that. And that's when—"

"The cops haul me out of school in cuffs on my first day off suspension."

"And they throw you in juvie," Gary says. "And that's when my lawyer starts trying to get me to match my story to Vaughn's. I tell him I'm not selling you out. No effing way!"

Gary takes a bite of his bar. Chews. Swallows. Grips the edge of the table with both hands. "That's when the lawyer says if me and Vaughn both tell the truth, then the only thing left for you to do is tell the truth too. He says if we all tell that same story, then the whole thing is over. And the best part is, he says you'd get way less time for coming clean. Something like mine and Vaughn's deal. At worst you'd get a couple months. Not a whole damn year and a half! Why wouldn't I believe him? I believed, believed, *believed* I was doing the best thing for you."

I bite into the side of my cheek.

"Your rookie lawyer didn't get the memo. Or he thought he was smarter than everyone else and he was gonna notch a win on his lawyer belt. So he didn't tell you to come clean. He fought for you instead. When he finally figured out you were gonna take the fall, the best he could do was cut that crappy deal you got. Me and Vaughn got sprung from juvie. And you got sent away to Zephyr Woods."

"A year and a half," I say. "Five hundred fifty-three days. Thirteen thousand hours."

"You think I haven't done that math a thousand times? You think I don't have a *Tonio calendar*? And I haven't been marking off every single day you been gone?"

He slides the tiny napkin out from underneath his maple bar. He unfolds it and blows his snot loud. "I'm sorry I ever asked you to help us rob Lance Cushman. I'm sorry me and idiot Vaughn got you sent away for so long and messed up your life. That was the exact opposite of my intentions. I am sorry for what I did to your heart. And to our friendship."

I nod my head like I'm listening.

"It's not gonna stop slowly eating my guts away forever," he says. More nodding.

"Like acid," he says. "Burning me up."

"That's good."

"FYI, that acid keeps me up at night."

"Uh-huh."

"You're right," he says, "I deserve it."

"Yup."

"But we got more to discuss, Tonio. I been waiting to make this thing right with you. Now here you are. And it's time for us to go dig up that—"

"Stop talking!" I lean across the table. "You been seeing Maya?"

"Of course," he says.

I'm about to lunge over the table when my phone buzzes. *Maya?*

WHERE ARE YOU?

It's Claudio!

I run for the door.

"I got two more minutes, Tonio! We gotta talk about the money!"

I reach for the handle and turn back. Grace is shaking her head, wondering what kind of trouble I'm in now. And sending me a message that we've got more to discuss.

"Thank you, Grace!"

"The money, Tonio!"

The door dings behind me as I sprint out onto Pac Highway. Gary Jr. and I still have unfinished business. But it has nothing to do with money.

When We Rescued Gary Jr.

So then... ninth-grade year,
under the moonlight of a cold October night,
we trespassed onto a moored yacht—The Mount Rainy-er.

We struck poses on the bow like victorious pirates
and gulped sodas we lifted from the galley fridge.

Staring into black Puget Sound, we fake-talked upper crust,
like the folks who owned Mount Rainy-er must.

> My good fellow, would you be so kind
> as to furnish me with another soda, the flavor of cherry-lime?

Maya shivered in the whipping wind.

> There's a polar bear plunge on the beach in the morning.
> What are people thinking? The water is freezing!

Gary Jr. straightened up in his puffy coat, beanie, and jeans.

He cleared his throat and said,

Maya, my dear, sometimes life
can become so dull, so boring,
it takes an ice-cold jolt to wake you up
and remind you that you are alive.

Gary Jr. was a little high. So he laughed and
laughed at the philosophical stuff he just said.

Maya and me, we laughed and laughed,
cuz Gary Jr. was hilarious when he was high.

He played hurt, shaking an angry fist at us.
Then, straight-faced, he turned to Maya.

Would you please be so kind
as to hold my Coca-Cola, madame?
So I may show you what living life to the fullest looks like?

Then he jumped off the back of the boat.

Maya and me quit laughing. Cuz we knew that in a minute,
Gary's jeans and puffy jacket would be sponging up water,
taking on weight, and pulling him down.

Swim to the boat, Gary!

I ripped a life ring off the wall and tossed it.

It landed close, but Gary couldn't see it.

He was too busy flailing, fighting the tide,
sinking, bobbing up, sinking, bobbing...

Each time he went under, it was for longer,
till eventually, Gary Jr. just didn't come up.

I finally reacted, feeling so stupid for laughing at Gary high.
Cuz me and Maya laughing could mean me and Maya losing Gary.

I peeled off layers and leaped!
And when my head went under,
I felt the immediate seaweed brain freeze.

I popped back up—YOWEEEEEEEEEEEEEEE!

And when I stopped screaming, I felt my feet touch muddy bottom.
I stretched and stood up tall,
my chin resting on the surface of the water.

    To your left! Maya shouted.

I reached under, searching, till at long last,
Gary's hand gripped mine.
I pulled and he pulled, and when his head popped up,
he was coughing and coughing.
I was shouting and shouting,

    Stand up! Stand up!

As we walked to the shore, Gary was chattering, his teeth clacking.

You saved my life! he shouted. I owe you forever!

In my mind, I thought, You don't owe me a thing, Gary,
cuz I needed that plunge, that ice-cold jolt.
And I needed the feeling I could do something good.

FRIDAY `11:55 PM`

Claudio steps out of the shadows and grabs me by the arm. He marches me around the back of the house, whispering the whole way. "Between Uber rides, I rest in the studio. The bush outside your room looked trampled. I tried the window. It slid right open."

"I'm sorry," I say. "I'm so sorry."

"Maya?"

"Gary Jr."

"What are you thinking? *Your curfew.* You broke parole."

"I know. It was stupid. I'm sorry."

"Your mom seems better," he says, "but stress kills. We can't mess with that. You, Antonio, may not mess with that."

"I'll explain it to her," I say. "You don't have to—"

"No!"

"No?"

"This is between us. You and me, we got a good thing here. Let's keep it that way."

I nod.

"Cuz your poor mom..." He reaches for my collar. Stops himself. Shoves his hands into his pockets. "I swear, Antonio. I swear if you so much as...oh my God, I will...not hesitate to..."

It's obvious he doesn't have it in him to hurt me or anyone else in this world.

"I don't know what I'd do. But I'm positive we would both regret it, so..."

He reaches and slides the window open. He bends at the knees. "Up you go." He locks the fingers of both hands together, making a loop for me to step into. And he boosts me up.

I look down at him. "Thank you."

"Shut up and go to bed."

"Thank you, thank you, thank you."

"This never happened," he says. "Tomorrow's a new day. Be good."

FRIDAY

SATURDAY

SUNDAY

MONDAY

A knock on the door. Claudio calls out, "*Pancakes!*"

I yawn huge. My head throbs after a sleepless night. Too much thinking about blowing it—my mom's trust in me, my future in this sweet little house, even my relationship with Claudio—all because of Gary Jr.

Too much crying, trying to figure out why Maya brushed me off. Too much desperate scheming about what I can do to get her to see me, to talk to me, to listen to me do step nine.

Too much tossing and turning got me nowhere but tired. It's time for a new strategy. A new plan for a new day. Sometime in the night, I realized I needed to be around some other messed-up, supportive people who might also need help getting through this day. I found a 10:00 AM AA meeting in the basement of St. Catherine's Episcopal Church, uphill on 188th, on the other side of Pac Highway. I shower, then make myself presentable in new jeans and a button-down shirt, then head to breakfast.

My mom's at the table feeding Olivia. Claudio is manning the stove, spatula in hand, humming an upbeat tune. He smiles big at me. "¿Dormiste bien?"

"Slept great." I yawn and stretch big. "That mattress, man. I tell ya. How 'bout you?"

"Nothing out of the ordinary," he says. "I was out till about three. Got a solid five hours of sleep. No complaints." He flashes a menacing wink and hands me a plate stacked high.

At the table, my mom keeps looking from me to Olivia to Claudio, beaming, like she still can't believe we're all together.

I bring up the AA meeting.

"Great!" she says. "Claudio can take you."

I tell her I could use the walk.

Her expression turns serious. Like she thinks maybe I'm scheming a way to see Maya.

"It's a fifty-minute walk," I say. "When I get there, I'll text a selfie. I'll text another one when the meeting gets out. I'll be here forty-five minutes after that. You'll know exactly where I am the whole time."

My mom looks to Claudio. He shrugs.

She turns to me. "How long are the meetings?"

I give myself a little cushion to make sure. "Hour and a half."

"Antonio," she says, "I trust you."

I glance at Claudio.

He shoots me another one of those winks.

I stretch my arm in front of me and take a selfie with the St. Catherine's sign in the frame. I send the text to my mom. Very responsible.

I send one to Officer Murdock with a note:

> AA at St Catherine's church. Des Moines. 188th St.

I walk down the steps, through the door, and into the basement. Low ceiling. Brown concrete floor. Musty old church furniture and the aroma of doughnuts and coffee.

A tall guy with a handlebar mustache and an old green Sonics hoodie greets me with a handshake. "Good to see you, friend."

A middle-aged woman in purple Lululemon sweats grabs a Styrofoam cup of coffee and a doughnut out of a Westernco box.

I close my eyes to get myself focused, cuz I'm gonna share today.

My name is Antonio. I got out of prison yesterday. I was sent there because . . .

I feel a hand on my back. I open my eyes. The Sonics-hoodie guy nods approval at my deep thinking. "Time to head in, bud."

There are a dozen metal chairs in a half circle. Another one for the chairperson.

An old lady with bluish hair and gold earrings is already at one end. She's sitting up, perfect posture, smiling like a kindergarten teacher on the first day of school.

I take a seat on the other end and close my eyes again. *Things were rough at home. I felt alone. I stayed out all hours drinking with my best friend. I needed money....*

Maybe instead of telling my story, I'll just listen. I'll stay after and ask the chairperson my questions. Like, *What if you know that making amends to a certain person would change* everything—*like, it would get you over a hump in your life—but that person doesn't even want to see you? How do you stop that from messing with your mind?*

When most of the seats are filled, Ellen, the chairperson, welcomes us to the meeting. She's about my mom's age. Spiky hair. A long, baggy sweater and black skinny jeans. She explains how the meeting will work. She reads the "Preamble," then hands things over to that morning's speaker, who happens to be blue-hair-gold-earrings lady.

Earrings lady was a straight-A nerd in high school. Party queen in college. Got married. Couldn't stop partying until she lost her husband and kids.

She's going on about her divorce when a man walks in late. From the corner of my eye, I notice the guy hesitate on the way to his seat on the other end of the half circle.

I'm thinking, *Is he looking at me?* Then I shake it off and refocus on the lady. But I swear the guy does a double take at me as he sits. I can't help but glance at him and...

My muscles turn to jelly. I lose my balance and slip off my chair. I catch it before it topples over, but it clangs and everyone turns my way to see what happened.

I sit, my heart *Psycho*-stabbing my chest from the inside out. I close my eyes again and fight to slow my breaths so I can think what to do.

I inhale as deep as I can.

Because that man—the man *smiling at me now,* the man who *winks at me*—is the one person I am not supposed to be anywhere near.

I exhale. Then stop because I have to think fast.

I glance at the door.

I need to run.

I can't move my legs.

I want to shout.

I don't have the air.

I can't unsee my dad. So unless I call Murdock...I sit up straight. Slide fingers into my pocket. Grip my phone like a gun.

Call Murdock!

Run!

Do something!

I'm stuck.

Frozen.

Staring.

At him. He smiles at me. He winks. He mouths the words

Good to see you! And he turns to face the blue-hair lady like all that—like running into me here, seeing me after all this time—was totally no-big-deal, nothing-to-see-here normal.

I sit up tall. Swallow hard. *Focus on the lady. Listen to the lady. Only the lady.* She quotes what her sponsor said about checking in even when things are going great.

I try not to. But I can't stop sneaking peeks at my dad. And noticing the difference. He's got weight to him. No red-drunk puffiness. He's tan. His blond hair short on the sides, wavy on top, like I remember from when I was a kid. He looks so young. And tall. He's wearing a light-blue shirt under a V-neck wool sweater. Fresh khakis. And that dopey smile he flashed me. So happy. As if our worst times never even happened. Like I'm five years old and he just got home from the Crypt with a stack of comics for us to read together.

Stop it, Antonio! Those memories are not him. Not the real Brad Sullivan.

I remember I texted Murdock. *He knows I'm here! What if he shows up?*

Stand, Antonio.

Stand up and run! Feet pushing into the floor. Leg muscles flexing. I'm about to. I'm going to. But earrings lady finishes her story and Ellen opens the meeting up for sharing.

My dad jumps right in and introduces himself to the group.

Everyone says, "Hi, Brad."

He says he's been sober for eight months, twenty-three days, twelve hours.

Stand, Antonio!

Run, Antonio!

I get a cheek lifted off my seat, but he turns to me. A bunch of alcoholics turn with him.

"I'm surprised my son is here with us today," he says. "I am so damn happy to see him." He closes his eyes. Inhales deep. Lets out a long, steady breath. And tells our story.

The happy beginning. Then my mom gets sick. He's overwhelmed. He starts drinking. He's scared. He's stressed. They fight. He hits her. He loses his business. She moves out. He deals drugs to keep us afloat. He hates himself. And he takes it out on me. Verbally. Physically.

"Antonio needed a lot of parenting," he says. "But whatever connection we had when he was younger, I trashed that."

My dad talks about how bad his father was with him. I never heard any of that before, because he didn't have a relationship with his dad and he never talked about him. Besides comics, he didn't talk about his childhood at all.

He turns to me again. All eyes on me again. I stare at a spot on the floor as he says, "I didn't keep food in the house for you. Didn't buy school clothes for you. Didn't think about where you were half the time. Most of the time. Maybe I was even relieved when you were out. I blamed you for what happened with your mother and me."

He says my arrest was a shock to his system. The shock he needed. His rock bottom. He fell completely to pieces. He was forced to stop. To think. To admit to himself that he was responsible for losing my mom. For losing me. And he had to seek help. To go to his first meeting. To take responsibility for his actions.

97

I look up from the floor. Glance his way. Our eyes lock.

"It was time to get my life together. I needed to make things right with the people I hurt."

Eyes back on the floor, I'm thinking how relieved I was when I thought it was over between us. But it's not over. Because he gets it. All the pain he caused. He's taking responsibility. Accepting blame.

I blame him for a lot. But I *do not* blame him for the crime I committed. That's on me. I made the choice to rip off Lance Cushman. It's my fault I ended up at Zephyr. My choices. No excuses. But to hear him admit that he played a role, admit that he put me in the position to even make a choice like that—it means something to me.

My dad finishes by telling how he's living his life now. He has a normal job, a new partner, a new life.

Ellen hands him a box of tissues. He wipes tears and finishes up by thanking God and all the alcoholics who listen to him tell his story every Saturday and Wednesday.

He turns to me and says, "Thank you for letting me be here with you."

I nod to my dad.

He smiles at me and turns to face the front.

As hoodie guy starts sharing, I try to figure out how to get outta here. Cuz no matter how nice it was to hear him say that stuff, I can't get caught with him. Do I say hi after? And tell him I gotta go? Then run? Do I stay in my chair and wait for him to walk out first?

I breathe to clear my head, trying to channel Mrs. Williams.

It doesn't work. Thankfully, the meeting comes to an end with the Serenity Prayer.

> God grant me the serenity
> To accept the things I cannot change;
> Courage to change the things I can;
> And wisdom to know the difference.

People walk out. Two or three stay to help Ellen fold and stack chairs. I put my head down, hoping for some serenity, courage, and wisdom. I sit hoping like that, waiting him out. It doesn't work, cuz I feel a tap on my shoulder.

"Hi, Antonio."

Before I can respond, Sonics-hoodie guy approaches us. He wants my chair.

I stand. He grabs it, then nods his head at us like, *I been there.*

My dad clears his throat. "I'm sorry, son. No way I could have known you'd be here."

I clear my throat. Swallow. Nod.

"I'm glad you were," he says.

"It's time, guys." Ellen's at the door with her hand on the light switch. "I have to lock up. Could you grab that last chair for me?"

When my dad turns to reach for the chair, I bust out of there.

Up the stairs. Down the hill. I run and run, my dad's voice, his words in my head, the image of us standing there together.

You can feel a twinge in your gut when things are not quite right. I don't feel the twinge. What I feel is my dad trying hard. Just like I'm trying hard. I think about how I don't want to be

99

judged for my past junk. I want to be judged for who I am now, an imperfect person trying to do the best that I can. Just like him.

A buzz in my pocket. I pull out my phone. *Murdock*.

Great! Keep the updates coming.
C u Mon at 7am.
ON TIME!!!

When the End of Us Came, It Sounded like Pounding

So then... summer after freshman year,
my dad slunk in smelling like booze.
Back collapsed against the door, sneering, glaring at us,
disgust painted on his face in red and shadows.

I turned away, emptying a syringe into my mom's hip,
a job he'd once done lovingly.

My dad took a step toward us and said,

> *I handed over the keys. The Crypt is closed for good.*

We stayed still. Didn't look. Said nothing.

He pounded a drumbeat on the door with his fist.
Boom! Boom! Boom!

I felt fear closing my throat. Squeezing my guts.

My mom grunted. Exhausted by him. Through with him.

His announcement and pounding
didn't accomplish the intended response.
So he walked fast past us, into the kitchen, through the door,
into my mom's studio, where drunken anger
powered a swinging arm, a hammer at the end of it.
Bang! Bang! Bang!
The rhythmic smashing of her wheel and kiln,
accompanied by his sobbing and shouting,
till there was nothing but hunks of bent metal and dust.

Soon enough, Tammy showed up
and moved my mom out of our place and into hers.

At best, me and my dad lived like strangers in that house.
At worst, we were predator and prey in that house.

So I spent days and nights,
as many as I could,
away.

I reach for the doorknob, but my phone buzzes. It's a text from my mom asking how I'm doing.

Breathe, Antonio.

I inhale deep.

I exhale slow, reminding myself there's no way she knows I saw him. Murdock couldn't possibly know. So everything's fine. It's good. I'm good. We're good.

I stand up straight. Take one more big breath. And walk inside.

She's sitting alone on the sofa, raising a finger to her smiling lips. My mom points at the bassinet on the floor. Then to a wall clock. She gives me a thumbs-up for making it on time.

I sit and watch Olivia breathing and think I could just do that and not do anything stupid for a long, long time. But my mom scoops Olivia into her arms and takes her to her crib.

I think about next steps. Because that meeting? It's over. Seeing my dad? Over. Seeing Gary Jr.? Over. Breaking curfew? Over. Worrying about Maya? Over. It's time to get my plan back on track. It's time to be *here*. Solidly just *here*. And it's time to do step nine with my mom.

I close my eyes. In my mind, I practice the lines just the way I wrote them. But when I get to the part where I apologize for stuff I did, I trip up. Because how can I apologize for the things I did before Zephyr Woods without apologizing for everything that's happened since I got home?

On the other hand, how would it come across if I straight-up look her in the eye and say, *Mom, I've only been home twenty-four hours, and I already texted Maya, trying to get her to meet up right after you told me I couldn't see her. I broke curfew and saw Gary Jr. And—oh yeah—Dad was at the AA meeting. I didn't leave. And I didn't call Murdock. So I broke your rules. And two parole terms. Sorry 'bout that!*

She plops down onto the sofa. Takes my hands into her palms, wraps them up, and squeezes.

I'm going to do it. I'm going to apologize. But leave out the new stuff.

She talks first. "¿Antonio, qué pasó después de la reunión?"

She knows! "Huh? What? After the meeting?"

"Uh-huh." Her eyebrows raise and she nods, waiting.

I lower my eyebrows and bite my lip like I'm really thinking. "What?"

"You sent a selfie before the meeting. But you didn't send one after."

"Oh!" I say. "Right! I am so sorry. I was just…the meetings get super deep, and I was all up in my head, and then I was so pumped to get home, I forgot. I promise that won't happen again."

"I understand," she says. "But things are different now." She says her relationship with Claudio is based on honesty. On communication and trust. "It's not just about me and Claudio, or about you and me. It's also about how we're going to raise Olivia."

How we're going to raise Olivia. The look in her eyes, the tone of her voice when she says that. She means I'm on team Olivia too. That puts the biggest lump in my throat.

"I know I can trust you. Right?"

"You can, Mamá."

"I do trust you. But I worry. I worried about you every day you were gone," she says. "Horrible as it was, I knew where you were. But now? When you walk out that door?" She wiggles her fingers in the air, making a nervous, wild-eyed face. "My mind just goes. It's preocupación sin límites. Infinite worrying. When you're a parent, you'll understand."

Olivia's bassinet sits empty. It won't be long before she's old enough to do the kind of stuff that got me into so much trouble. I think I understand this concept of infinite worrying.

All this talk makes me want to come clean about what happened at the meeting. And about last night. I'm going to tell her everything. I really am.

But my mom's eyes are telling me she wants us to move forward. Not back. "I'll communicate," I say. "I'll be honest. You can trust me."

She holds her arms out for a hug. I go for it. I squeeze tight. She squeezes back. I'm hit with a warm wave of her love. And in my mind, and in my heart, I promise that from here on out I will be the person I need to be. I will not lie. I will not be a fraud.

She pulls away, covers her mouth, and yawns big.

I follow with one of my own.

"Estás cansado."

"You too, Mamá."

"I'm fine," she says. "I'm just going to do some laundry—"
She yawns another huge one.

I do again too.

"Duerme una siestita," she says.

In a second, her eyes are closed and she's breathing deep.

I go to the kitchen to grab some water. That's when I see an envelope on the counter by the fridge. *Premiere Northwest Hospital Alliance.* I pick it up. It's open. A bill. An overdue notice. *Holy hell!* I count each digit to make sure I saw it right.

Yup. Six freaking figures.

SATURDAY 10:00 PM

After a day of rocking Olivia and reading board books and changing the first diaper in my life...after watching way too much TV...after failing to find the right moment to do step nine and failing to ask my mom what's going to happen with that impossible hospital bill...after a mind-blowing pasta-and-sauce dinner made by Claudio...after more TV...

I settle into my cozy bed again. I stretch and yawn. Pull covers up tight. Close my eyes.

Bzzt-bzzt! Bzzt-bzzt!

I reach in the dark for my phone. I check the caller. I see the name. But I can't believe it.

Bzzt-bzzt! Bzzt-bzzt!

I shouldn't. I can't. I'm not going to.

That parole term. Did it say, *You may not "see" your father?* Or, *You may not "have contact with" your father?*

I breathe in deep as I cock my thumb to hang up.

I exhale slow, staring at the screen.

He was so good at the meeting. He was healthy.

Bzzt-bzzt! Bzzt-bzzt!

Trying so hard. What if this is an emergency?

Bzzt-bzz—I pick up.

"Antonio?" he says.

"Yeah?"

"I didn't think you'd—"

"It's okay, Dad." *It's not okay.*

"I'm sorry I was at the meeting," he says. "I mean, I'm sorry I stayed when I saw you."

"It's fine, Dad." *It's not fine.*

But it's not horrible. My dad sharing his story at an AA meeting? My dad calling me to apologize? I don't think that's what they had in mind when they came up with that parole term.

"You doing all right, Antonio?"

"Yeah."

"All settled in?"

"Uh-huh."

It's quiet on the other end.

"Darndest thing," he says. "I ran into that buddy of yours last week. What's his name?"

"Gary Jr.?"

"Just curious—has he mentioned me asking him about you guys? And the robbery?"

"Um, you know, Dad, I really shouldn't have picked up. So let's just—"

"Did he tell you I asked him about that money?"

"Haven't seen him. Haven't talked to him. It's all in my past, so—"

"Of course it is."

"All right, then."

"It's just—Nancy and me," he says, "we watch *Law and Order* all the time—*Criminal Intent* and *Special Victims Unit*. And that PBS show. The British one. Tip of my tongue... It's got that vicar detective. You know it?"

"I don't even know what a vicar—"

"It's just, when you watch those shows, you can't help but, subconsciously, you know, start seeing mysteries in everything. It makes you real curious. You ever get super curious about something like that?"

"Uh-huh."

"That's all that was."

"All what was?"

"I'll back up," he says. "When your buddies got caught after robbing Lance, they had cash on them. But it wasn't all of it. There was more. A lot more. And no one knows where it is."

"I don't either."

"Of course you don't. That's not what I'm—it's just, you know, that detective mindset kicking in. And you're like, *Where could that much money disappear to?*"

"I have to go, Dad."

He laughs. "I must have been a private eye in another life, right?"

I want to put an end to this. So I tell him everything I know. Gary Jr. and Vaughn were supposed to bury the money out east, past North Bend, up at Rattlesnake Lake. The plan was, we'd all go back in a few days and retrieve it, when we thought it was safe. I figured Gary and Vaughn were pulled over before they even got to North Bend.

"I never heard about missing money," I say. "How do *you* know about it?"

"Lance Cushman," he says. "He called me from prison. He's losing it, stewing in his toxic juices, obsessing over money he'll never see again. Serves him right."

"Okay, Dad."

"You know what? I bet the cops took it. The money. They do that kind of thing."

"I gotta go, Dad."

"Right. Me too. And, Antonio?"

"Yeah?"

"Thanks for talking. And thanks for the meeting. Means a lot to me that you stayed."

I should hang up. But I ask him if he has any of my stuff.

He says he's still got some old boxes. Comics and toys. Some clothes.

"Have you seen my Forlán jersey?"

"Oh, I don't know. You're welcome to come over and—"

"Better not."

"Know what? I'll talk to your mom. We'll work out how to get you those boxes."

"Maybe don't call her," I say. "Not for a while."

"Got it. And I won't talk about that money anymore. Sorry I even brought it up."

"We shouldn't talk at all. Not until I'm through with parole."

"You're right," he says. "But you know what? Keeping you on the phone plan was worth it just for this conversation. Should I keep paying that?"

My dad got me a phone when he forced me to make deliveries. He's been paying for it ever since without saying a word. I quit thinking about it. I know I can't be on his plan now. But I need my phone. "Maybe one more month?" I say. "That'll give me time to switch to Mom's plan."

"Sounds good to me," he says. "And, Antonio?"

"Yeah?"

There's silence on the line for a while. Then he says, "Take care, son."

"You too, Dad." We finally hang up. I take a big gulp of air. I try to release it real slow, but before I'm done, the phone rings again. I pick it up. "What, Dad?"

"You talked to your dad? What the literal effing eff, Tonio?"

"I blocked your cell. I blocked your landline. What number are you calling me from?"

"Oh bud, my bud," Gary says, "we been through too much for too long to let some blocked numbers get in the way of our friendship."

"Bye, Gary."

"There's a party tonight."

"I don't care."

"It's at Amanda's."

"I'm not going."

"Pick you up in the mini truck."

"You will not."

"Eleven oh seven at the 7-Eleven."

"Nope."

"Maya's gonna be there."

When, Wrapped Up in Each Other, We Did Not Kiss

So then . . . fall of sophomore year,
Maya and me dug out the dry bags we'd stashed
under the limbs and boards of the driftwood pile.

We unzipped and opened them up, pulling out tarps,
blankets, dry sweatshirts, hoodies, and socks.
And soon we were wrapped up cozy and squeezing hands.

The tapping of raindrops on planks.
The plipping of raindrops in water.
The blopping of raindrops on mud.

There would be no beach walk in this weather.
So this was it. I could feel it. It had to be.
The night I was gonna kiss Maya.

We lay there, face-to-face.
Maya smiling at me, her brown eyes mischievous.

I swallowed the lump in my throat and leaned in

just as Maya rolled to the side, reaching for her backpack
and pulling out a bottle of vodka
she'd swiped from her mom's latest guy.

Wanna try? she asked.

Better not, I said.

She unscrewed the cap. Closed her eyes. Took a swig.

Ugh, she said. It tastes like paint.
But it feels so good going down.

The way she looked at me, her eyes pleading me to try.

I took the bottle and tilted it, the vodka disgusting on my tongue.
But this night was cold, and the stuff warmed me up.

We passed that bottle back and forth,
back and forth, till Maya asked,

How'd we get here?
We met at the crack in the sidewalk, I said.
Then we raced down the hill, holding hands.

She punched my shoulder.

No, stupid! How'd we turn into kids who get wasted
and don't sleep at home on a school night?

Are we bad, Maya?

I laughed and laughed at that, then knocked that bottle back.

She shoved me hard, her whole body hard, her eyes hard on mine.

Yes, Antonio, she said, we are bad.

Maya gazed into the darkness
as we listened to the sound of waves gliding gently in,
the tide pulling them out God-strong.

She scooted close and rested her head on my chest.
I wrapped an arm around her, inhaling the smells of her hair and salt.

Maya's hands and fingers gripped my fingers tight,
her body burrowing into mine, as we fought to get closer,
closer, closer, when closer was impossible.

The first of so many nights of us, best friends
drunk and wrapped up in each other,
keeping warm until the sun came up
and the tide chased us away.

"Oh, Tonio, herefore art thou, Tonio! In the Mazda mini truck of your dreams!" Gary pulls us out of the 7-Eleven parking lot. As wrong as it is, it feels good to be in this rusted-out truck again. A seat spring pokes my butt like old times. The smell of motor oil, weed, and fake pine from the many green-tree air fresheners hanging from his mirror. Until Maya got her old red Civic, we never had cars, so Gary would give us rides at all hours. One night when he was too stoned to drive, he taught me how to clutch and to shift gears and I managed to get us home.

Gary reverses and spins the truck around. He takes a right onto Pac Highway and pulls an illegal U-turn at the light. "You and me two nights in a row, Tonio! That's good, cuz we got business to discuss."

"Let's get this straight," I say. "Tonight is not about you and me. It's not about our past. It's about me and Maya. And please do not tell her I know she's coming."

"I gotta be honest," he says. "Maya said she'd *probably* show up.

So that's, like, ninety-five percent she'll be there? Just be aware of that five percent."

I tell him if I get caught sneaking out but I didn't get to see Maya, I'm coming after him.

He says Maya's been showing up lately. She says hi and sips on a Coke. Fifteen, thirty minutes later, she takes off.

"She's drinking Coke and...?"

"Coke and nothing. She's been living that sober AA life."

I tell Gary I'm in AA too, so I won't be drinking a drop at this party either.

"That's cool," he says. "You can smoke weed, though, am I right?"

"Sorry, man. The law. Parole terms. AA. You know."

"I struggle with the logic," he says. "But I respect your path."

Half a block from Amanda's, we park and walk toward the thumping bass. Gary Jr. leads us through a side door of the house and down a set of stairs to the basement, where Tall Dominic tends the keg, just like old times. Dom pours one for Gary Jr.

Gary stands on his toes and shouts at Dom over the music. "None for Tonio!"

Tall Dom nods and gives me a thumbs-up.

Gary heads toward the stairs. I tell him to hold up. And I ask Dom to pour half a red cup.

"You sure?" he says.

"Nah, a third of a cup."

We take a seat in white plastic chairs by the chain-link fence in the backyard. The *thump-thump* is muffled enough that we can hear each other.

Gary points at my cup. "You sure about that?"

"It's not to drink. Just to hold."

I ask him if he can text Maya.

He pulls out his phone.

Without even thinking, I bring the cup to my lips. But as soon as I get a whiff of that keg-beer smell, I pull it away and set it down between the legs of my chair.

"Close call," Gary says.

AA-wise, I'm still okay cuz I haven't taken a sip. But if Murdock showed up, I'd be toast. But what are the chances? There are a million people living between his home up in Seattle and here. Hundreds of neighborhoods. Thousands and thousands of houses.

Gary checks his phone. Shoves it in my face. There's a message from Maya.

Coming over. Won't stay long.

"It's good she's coming," he says. "She's missing you bad."

"She is?" I say, my heart skipping beats. "Really?"

"Yeah, you big dope. All she does is talk about you."

"What about you and her?" I say.

"What *about* me and her?"

I wipe sweat off my forehead. "You know what I mean, *GJ*."

"Are you asking if me and Maya...?"

"Yes!"

"Bud! Seriously. Whoa. Just. Stop."

"So, you and Maya?"

"My God, Tonio! Me and her text. We talk sometimes. We see each other at parties for, like, a minute. That's it."

"You sure?"

"I'm gonna spell this out in terms you can comprehend," he says. "Is Maya cool and funny and smart? Yes, she is. Does she make you feel like you are the most important person in the world whenever she says your name? She does. Is it super cute when she talks about fish? It is. But *come on!* What are you even thinking? What you and her have, Tonio, it's too deep for anyone else to come between, so it's never even crossed my mind. Not one time."

"What else? Something happened between you two."

"Only thing we did is hang out at Westernco four or five times a few months ago. But all we did was talk about you and about her fight to get stable. She has stories, Tonio. Some super-rough times after you went away."

I ask him what he means.

"That's up to her to explain."

"How long has it been since she texted?"

"Don't worry, she'll be here. In the meantime, we got urgent matters to discuss."

"I told you I'm not talking about money or the past. Got it?"

"Got it. I'm gonna respect your wishes, Antonio."

I turn to check the street for Maya.

"Cuz our relationship is all about that respect."

"Right, Gary."

"But I'll tell you one thing. The cash isn't at Rattlesnake Lake. Cuz me and Vaughn never made it there."

A shout comes from the street. "Jesus Christ, Gary!"

When Looking in His Eyes,
I Saw the Worst I Was

My dad took gig jobs but struggled hard.
He felt he didn't stand a chance.
So winter, my sophomore year,
he went to work for his old buddy Lance.

Whatever the job, it couldn't be good,
cuz the cash came in paper bags.
When I asked, he wouldn't tell,
he just slapped me and yelled, Never nag!

So I stayed away when he might be home,
until one day in early spring,
I walked in and there he was.

> *He said, I need you to do this thing.*

He handed me a slip, Lance's address.
And stuffed a bag in my pack.

> *He said, Exchange it with Lance's.*

You gotta go fast. You have one hour to get it back.

I walked half an hour, then knocked on his door,
hating being at Lance's place.
He opened up, ripped the bag away,
then slammed the door in my face.

I stood stuck cuz of what might happen
if I returned to my dad empty-handed.
Before I knew it, Lance was back
and he stuffed a new bag in my pack.

I counted, he said. It better all be there
when you hand that bag to your dad.

What is it?

That's cash, dear boy,
cuz your dad is a seller of drugs.
Now you're one too. I'm sure he's proud
that his son is a little thug.

I turned to go, then immediately froze
at the sight of a too-skinny guy.
He was pockmarked, looking zombie lost,
and as he shuffled, he brushed by my side.

He stopped and turned, and I caught his eyes.
And those eyes, they gazed straight through mine.

121

Then a shiver shot from the top of my head
all the way down the length of my spine.

I hated Lance, I couldn't stand my dad
for turning a man into that,
and I hated myself for standing there
and holding that paper sack.

That hate just grew, it multiplied fast,
because me delivering sacks?
That was just the start. I couldn't say no.
It went on and on like that.

SATURDAY `11:43 PM`

Maya's standing inside the backyard gate. Arms folded. Eyes welling. Freckles burning.

But *my God*. Her face has filled out. There's color in her cheeks. She's standing tall. Her wavy black curls are full and long.

I went away. And Maya got better. I got subtracted from her, and she became more.

She points at me and spits words at Gary. "Did you tell him I was coming?"

"What's not a lie is I didn't tell him you weren't *not* coming."

She throws the gate open and rushes through, out onto the sidewalk, toward her car.

Gary punches my shoulder. "If you love her, go after her!"

"Shut up, Gary!" I run across the lawn, out the gate. "I'm sorry, Maya!"

She turns to me. "I told you I'd see you when I was ready!"

"You said I should see *Gary*. So I did. He just now told me you might be showing up."

"I don't believe you," she says, shaking her head like she doesn't know me anymore. Then she waits, hoping I have a better explanation.

I have so much to say. Too much. I can't get the words to come.

Maya grunt-huffs and rolls her eyes, waving me off like she was stupid for expecting I might say something worthwhile. She turns away and reaches for the car door.

"Wait. Please, Maya. Just give me a minute."

"Nope," she says, marching my way. "I talk. You listen. Sit." She points to the curb.

I sit.

She breathes in deep. Tilts her head back and exhales. Then she sits. Close but not too close. She pulls up bits of grass. Tosses them into the street. "I wanted to see you, Antonio. I didn't know when or where. But I'll tell you one thing. Not in the middle of the night. Not at a party at Amanda Hoover's."

I got no response.

For the longest time, it's just the sound of muffled party noises and the rumble of jets taking off from Sea-Tac.

Finally, she turns to me. "Things were bad before. At home. But I had you. We could run away from our problems together. Drink them away together. Then you were gone."

She rehashes the part of her story I already know. Her mom had really struggled. There were men coming and going all the time. Maya lived in a house that didn't feel like her home.

Then she says stuff I didn't know. Like after I went away, she quit feeling like alcohol filled the void. She tried new stuff. Anything she could get her hands on. She felt out of control.

Maya doesn't get specific but says she ended up spending nights out alone. Her face is a wreck when she says one of those nights was rock bottom.

That was the night she decided to get clean. She got into treatment. Talked to her mom about needing stability. She needed *her*. Rhonda responded. Got some help of her own. Now they're doing good together. And Maya has sober friends and a sponsor supporting her. Some nerd friends she studies with after school. Things are looking up.

"Money's tight," Maya says. "We might move in with my grandma in Bremerton."

"What about school and your meeting and your friends?"

"It's okay," she says. "We'll figure it out."

"If there's anything I can—"

"Uh-uh," she says, shaking her head like it's not my job.

I stop talking. But I can't stop thinking I want to be the one to make things better for her.

Maya turns to full-on face me, her eyes focused hard on mine. "Okay," she says, "here goes."

Here goes what?

"When we spent nights out at the pier, I always brought the alcohol. I thought we were escaping. We weren't. We were just running to something else that only made our lives harder. I made *your life* harder. If it wasn't for me, maybe things would have turned out different for you."

"That's not—"

"Let me finish. I'm sorry. For all that. I'm truly sorry. And I promise, when the time comes that we start hanging out again, if things get hard, we'll work through it. We won't run."

It hits me what just happened. "Was that step nine?"

"Yeah."

"That's bullshit, Maya!"

"What is?"

"You have nothing to be sorry for! You didn't force me to drink. I made that choice every single time. *I chose* not to put a stop to it. *I chose* to take Gary Jr. up on his stupid idea to rob Lance. *I chose* to plan the whole thing. And because of a stupid choice *I made*, I wasn't there for you anymore. I was gone. And none of that is on you. It's all on me."

Maya pulls up more grass, nodding, like thinking deep about what I just said.

"I did AA at Zephyr," I say.

"The kind of AA where it's okay for you to drink?"

"What are you talking about?"

"I saw the red cup under your seat."

"That was just for holding."

"You think I'm stupid?"

"Ask Gary!"

"Don't worry about it," she says, like it's not worth it.

"The point is, I was so angry about getting locked up. So angry about everything that got me there. I was lost in that anger."

I tell Maya I made promises in my mind to her. Like how I'd be a better friend to her. A better listener. Not so selfish. I tell her how much the thought of stuff like that—the thought of being together again—helped me get through the days. It was thoughts of her that helped me earn my parole and get released six months early.

I tell her I'm making small goals now, like being on time to my meeting at Puget Monday morning. I tell Maya how me and Mrs. Lucrisia are going to plan things out, how I'm dedicating myself to getting back on track just like she did. I'm focused on graduating and figuring out what needs to come next.

I wait for her voice again.

All I hear is distant dogs barking. The white noise of Pac Highway traffic. A rumble as another Sea-Tac jet rockets into the sky.

Maya. Is. Not. Responding.

"That's good," I say, not knowing what's good, or why I said it.

"You're living with your mom?" she says. "How is she?"

"Maya, she is so much—" I realize I forgot the biggest news. "I'm a big brother!"

Maya lights up. Her smile. Her cheeks. "How could you not lead with that?"

"Still getting used to it. Olivia Echeverría Hernandez. She's almost five months old."

"And the dad is..."

"Claudio Hernandez. They met at Albertsons. Super-nice guy. An amazing cook."

"You were saying about your mom?"

"She's bouncing around. She's funny. She's not even sick anymore."

"Oh my God, Antonio! Your mom is good. You're living with her. You have a sister." She punches me in the shoulder. "You better be the best big brother! You better treat that little girl like she's gonna be amazing. Like she deserves to be."

I drop my eyes to the ground. I fight to catch my breath. "I will. I promise."

"Hey," she says. "Look at me." She's smiling, her cheeks red, full, happy. "Antonio Sullivan, I believe you." And she says it like she's finally seeing me the way I see her. The way we used to see each other.

But this time we're not drunk.

I swallow.

She swallows.

I study her face, her eyes.

She studies mine.

She closes her eyes.

I close mine.

I lean way in.

She jerks back, her eyes popping open. "What—what are you doing?"

"I was just, uh—*oh no*—I thought—"

"Nope," she says, shaking her head. "Huh-uh."

I turn away fast. "Oh God, Maya. Oh hell. I didn't mean—I am so sorry."

"Antonio," she says, "that is not where we're headed. You hear me? Not for a long time. Maybe never." She stands up and walks to her car door. Reaches for the handle. "I'm glad things are good with your mom. Say hi. Hug your sister for me. And you be good. I'll call you. When the time is right. When I'm ready."

"Come on, Maya!"

"When I got your text, I felt this pull," she says. "I honestly thought about scoring booze and heading to the pier together. Like picking up right where we left off."

"I understand," I say.

"Understand *what*?" she says. "How messed up our friendship got?"

"No! I don't want to go back to that. I'm clean. I have goals. I'm on a path, Maya!"

"I can't trust you," she says.

"You just told me you believed me."

"That was before you tried to kiss me."

"I'll show you. I'll prove myself to you."

"I love you, Antonio!" She shakes her head like loving me is stupid. "But we are shit for each other."

Before I can respond, she opens up and hops in.

I run around to her side. I tap the window, begging her to stay and talk. Begging her to listen. Begging for another shot.

My mind is like, *Stop.*

Step away.

Breathe.

Smile.

Let her go.

But my heart... "Please, Maya! Please, let's just—can we start this conversation over? Stay, Maya! Talk to me, Maya! Please!"

She starts the car. Cracks the window. "Go away, Antonio!"

I hop to the front. Press my hands on the hood. I'm yelling right at the windshield, right at Maya, so she can hear me through the glass. Yelling ridiculous stuff—pounding on the hood now. "I'm changed! I'm better! Talk to me!"

Her eyes say, *You're scaring me. I don't know you.* She buries her face in her hands.

I rush back to her window. "I'm sorry, Maya. I'm sorry. I'm so sorry."

She looks up at me, tears streaming down her face. Then she pounds the gas and hauls out of there without looking back.

And I'm standing alone in the middle of the street as sounds whoosh in. Laughter from the party. Streetlights buzzing. Dogs barking. And Murdock's voice in my mind telling me I'm getting sent back to Zephyr for breaking curfew two nights in a row.

I get my ass moving. But before I make it to the end of the block, the mini truck is honking right behind me. I turn to see Gary Jr. pop his head out the window.

"Hop in, man!"

FRIDAY

SATURDAY

SUNDAY

MONDAY

I don't have energy for the argument. I get in the mini truck.

Gary nudges my shoulder. "What ever happened to Tonio Sullivan and Maya Jordan?"

I slam my fist into the dash. Kick my heels into the floor.

Breathe, Antonio.

Inhale deep, Antonio.

"I can't!"

"Are you talking to me?" Gary asks.

I shake my head. Then I close my eyes and try to take in a breath.

But Gary puts a hand on my shoulder. "I'm thinking Maya just needs a little spa—"

"Shut up, Gary!"

"I got weed. I think it might—"

"Shut up! Shut up!"

"Fine. No weed. You keep on inhaling that *regular* air. It's working awesome for you."

I glare daggers at him.

"Let's stick a pin in that weed topic," he says. "In the meantime, I'm going to say the last word regarding what happened that night with me and idiot Vaughn."

I roll down the window. Lean my face to catch the wind and try to shut him out.

"So we walk right into Lance's because the key works."

"I know it works, Gary! Otherwise there's no robbery!"

"Exactly. We go directly to the alarm keypad. It's right where you said it would be. Awesome, right? Not awesome, because that Vaughn insists on punching in the code."

I sit up, leaning my chest and face all the way out and into the wind. Like dogs do.

So Gary shouts. "The stress of the moment gets to Vaughn. He can't punch the code in right. He pokes the keypad over and over, harder and harder, until his beefy finger literally smashes a number—I think it was the seven—right through the pad, all the way to the wall. He manages to pull his finger out of the hole and, *BEE-BAW! BEE-BAW!* That alarm is howling, man! But we figure we still got a minute, so—"

"I don't want to hear it, Gary!"

"Believe me, you do. We get in the safe no prob. We're grabbing cash fast. We're grabbin' it and grabbin' it, hand over fist, and we're like, *Hold the phone! How much freaking money is there?* More than you told us there would be, Tonio. Cuz it's not only in the safe—there's Nike shoeboxes piled up all over the place. Vaughn spots the Jordans he's been coveting forever, in his exact size. He opens the box. No kicks. *Cash.* I couldn't believe it."

I grip the door handle. I swear I'm gonna jump out of this moving car.

"So we're on our way out with two trash sacks of cash on our backs. That's when Vaughn decides to make a run for it. However, as open as the front door was, Lance's storm door was closed tight. And it was clean glass from top to bottom. You can imagine where the story is headed."

"My God, please don't say—"

"Yup. Vaughn explodes through that glass door. Shattered glass flying everywhere. He doesn't stop running till he's sitting in the truck, dripping blood off his forehead like a leaky faucet. I pop the bags in back and drive away fast. And I'm trying to think straight, Tonio! But big-baby Vaughn is like, *I don't wanna stash the money. I can't wait. I wanna take my share now!*"

"Stop the truck, Gary."

"In a sec."

"Right now!"

"I tell him, *No, Vaughn!* But he won't stop that blabbering. I can't take it! I gotta quiet him down. So I pull over and get out of the truck and grab two shoeboxes out of a bag. I tie the bag back up, get in the truck, and hand the boxes over to Vaughn. As you will come to understand, that is a decision I would too soon regret."

I regret his stupid decision too. Because after hearing Vaughn's story in juvie, the cops searched our house and found a gun and a Nike shoebox stuffed with cash that my dad chose to hide under my bed. When Lance was arrested, they asked him about me because of the matching shoeboxes. He told them all about me running those sacks of cash and drugs for him. But he never mentioned my dad. It was the gun and drug-dealing charges, plus planning the robbery, that got me the two years in Zephyr.

"Anyways, cuzza that alarm, we nix the trip out to Rattlesnake and bury the bags at the marina under the cover of darkness. We're home free, right? Not so fast, because Vaughn's forehead is still bleeding bad. I know I talk a lotta smack about that idiot, but Vaughn is a good friend. So I gotta stop that blood flow. I fumble all over the truck for a rag, for a tissue, a paper towel, a doughnut napkin. . . . I find none of these items. Therefore, I—"

"Don't say it."

"—grab a fistful of dollars out of a shoebox and hand them to Vaughn so he may apply direct pressure to the wound. You following, Tonio?"

"Yes, Gary, I'm following."

"Turns out Lance's neighbors call the cops after hearing the alarm. They don't get my plates. But they give a decent description. So we get stopped. Right away, it's clear to the officers that they have their men, because the hundred-dollar bill glued by blood to Vaughn's forehead leads them to the eleven thousand four hundred and sixty-five dollars in the Nike Air Jordan shoeboxes tucked under the seat."

"Oh my God, Gary! What is the point of telling me all that now?"

"The point? Getting caught was all Vaughn's fault! But the good part is—"

"There is no good part!"

Gary pulls the truck over. He kills the engine. "The good part is they thought that was all the money. They don't know there's *way more* money out there."

"Who doesn't know?"

"The cops. The judge. The lawyers."

"Where did the money go?"

"I told you. It's at the marina."

"*Then* what happened to it?"

"The money is—read my lips, slowpoke—*buried...at... the...marina.*"

"How much?" I kick myself for asking.

"The twelve K they caught us with was in those shoeboxes. But those big bags we buried at the marina...if they were any more full, they'd split right open."

An image of bags bulging with cash pops into my head.

I shake the image away. "I'm done with that money," I say. "I'm done with Vaughn." Then before I can stop and think how to put it less harsh, I just spit the words out. "You too, Gary. I'm done with you. We are finished. We are over. Right now."

He turns to me, tears rolling. "That's not true, Tonio," he says, wiping his eyes. "You're my best friend. And you don't wanna admit it, but I'm your best friend too."

I can't take seeing Gary Jr. cry. I can't take him talking about us like that. I have to turn away and look out the window.

He starts up the truck and drives in silence.

And that silence lasts about half a minute, because Gary picks up the miserable story right where he left off.

After they're released from juvie, Vaughn begs Gary to dig up the money. He says he needs it immediately to buy a Boston

Whaler and supplies for a trip he's gonna take up the Salish Sea with his best friend, Charlie. Charlie, who we've always known is Vaughn's imaginary friend because of all the wild sci-fi stuff Vaughn says Charlie does. *Charlie made a lie-detector app. Charlie made a robot that can dig for clams. Charlie made a glitter bomb and set it off from the bottom of the ball pit at Chuck E. Cheese.* It's just too sad, all the stories that Vaughn makes up.

Anyways, Vaughn needs Gary to show him where the money is because the night they buried it, he was woozy from losing blood. Plus, it was dark and he'd never been to the marina.

Gary insists to Vaughn that they're gonna wait for me to get out of Zephyr. Gary holds him off so long that Vaughn is no longer even in the picture because his grandma ships him off to live with his retired-marine uncle in San Diego.

"It's me and you now, Tonio, and enough money to change our lives forever, just sitting there waiting for us." He kills the headlights as we glide to a stop a block from my mom's house.

I reach for the door handle.

"I'm getting shovels tomorrow morning," Gary says. "Tomorrow night we meet up at the marina gate. I take you to the spot. And we dig up those bags."

"I'm not gonna do it, Gary."

"I'm finally gonna make my movie dreams come true," he says. "I'm not moving to Portland anymore. I'm doing it right here in South King County. With legit gear. Are you familiar with the Red Komodo 6K S35?"

"I am not."

"It's the best camera on the market. And I am buying one. I'm buying lights, bounce boards, mics, booms, green screens, and everything I need for editing. Final Cut Pro, Pro Tools, giant monitors, multi-terabyte hard drives. And I'm paying these starving Seattle actors *scale*, man! They're not gonna know what hit 'em. Do you know what my movie's gonna be about?"

"I'm tired, Gary."

"Guess."

"I can't even—"

"The story of our lives, Tonio. You, me, Maya. Even idiot Vaughn."

"Wow. Just wow."

Gary taps his temple. "I got the screenplay all up here. Just waiting till I can put cash down on Final Draft Twelve. I'll boot that software up, let my fingers dance and the words flow."

"Good luck with that." As much as I want him out of my life, I truly want the best for Gary. But I'm so exhausted, my words come out sarcastic.

"You don't think I can do it," he says, staring right at me, his face burning red.

"I don't *think* you can do it, Gary. I *know* you can do it."

"No, you don't," he says, dropping his head onto the steering wheel.

I wait for more words. But it's silent in the truck.

I could leave Gary Jr. right now. He's giving me the chance to go.

But something keeps me in my seat.

It's just the sound of our breathing until Gary pops upright. "I'm gonna show you, Tonio!" He slaps the dashboard. "I'm gonna show my mom and dad. I'm gonna show every teacher who ever got frustrated with my ADHD mouth and treated me like an annoying problem that wasn't worth solving."

"You show 'em, Gary."

"I will! Now, go get that money with me!"

"I'm not going anywhere near it."

"I owe it to you."

"You don't owe me anything."

He hops off the seat, slapping the dash again. "Can't we be epic together, Tonio? For once in our lives? Is that too much to ask?"

I pull the door handle.

He stops me with a hand on my shoulder. "Fine. But I'm calling you tomorrow. We'll talk it over when your head isn't clouded by the fog of Maya."

I want this to be easier. Because Gary Jr. is kind. Gary Jr. is hilarious. Gary Jr. is inspiring. Doesn't matter. I gotta put my foot down. "You've been a true friend. I love you, man. But we're shit for each other. I'm sorry, Gary. This is goodbye. Forever."

I hop out, shut the door, and walk.

Gary Jr. drives at my side for the whole block.

When it's time for me to turn into the house, I can't help it. I sneak a peek at him.

"Bro!" he shouts, leaning over to the passenger window, his face exploding into laughter. "You almost had me there! For real you almost did!"

He steps on the gas and pulls away, shouting out his open window. "Two AM, Tonio! We're gonna be epic!"

I watch, shaking my head as the mini truck disappears around a corner. He's pretending it's not true. But this is one hundred percent the last time I have anything to do with Gary Jr.

I send a wish to the universe that he be kept safe and taken care of. And that all his dreams come true. And I have to admit, I'm gonna miss him. But the drama? I can't have it. Saying goodbye to Gary Jr. forever is a big relief.

Maya is a whole other story. I think about us being over. And I feel like I'm falling and I don't know how to catch myself.

I try breathing deep, but there's not enough air in the world to make me feel better about me and Maya Jordan.

When Mixing Fireworks and Wine, We Laughed

So then, spring break, sophomore year,
Maya, me, and Gary made our way to the pier,
loaded down with Red Vines, boxed wine,
convenience-store slices—pepperoni and Hawaiian—
and microwave popcorn that bulged a plastic trash bag.

And a bunch of bottle rockets, left over from summer,
that Gary swiped from his dad's closet stash.

We waded in the water, licorice hanging out our mouths,
netting bullheads and jellyfish, splash-fighting
and sloppy-sipping that wine.

We gulped and chugged, laughing and laughing,
as Gary Jr. launched missiles from his fist.
They whistled—FEEEEEEEEE-OOOOOOOOOOOO—
then landed in the sound with a hisssss.

Maya wanted to shoot one too.
Giggling silly, she wrestled Gary for the lighter,

not sober enough to notice
the kid had a grip on a bottle rocket he'd just lit.

Gary's fist got flung. The rocket shot straight up.
And the FEEEEEEEEEEE was not followed by an
OOOOOOOOO. It was followed by an UHK!
cuz the rocket found a pier-plank knothole
and got stuck.

Next thing we knew, we heard a sizzle.
We saw the smoke, then a spark, then flames.

We froze at first, stunned, just watching,
maybe hoping, that the fire might put itself out.

Gary took action. He grabbed the wine box.
Wedged it under his arm. He aimed, squeezed,
firing a pink stream at the plank.

Bull's-eye! And the flames exploded wider.

    Alcohol makes it worse! Maya shouted.
    Throw mud!

Gary watched in shock as me and Maya tossed mud.
We tossed it and tossed it, until that plank and the two of us
were totally covered and the flames shrank
and there was nothing left but smoldering smoke.

We had saved the Des Moines Marina Pier from utter destruction. And we laughed in relief, and because we thought it was funny.

Don't worry, guys, Gary said,
I got one more box of rockets.

Don't worry, guys, Maya said, I got one more box of wine.

SUNDAY `8:22 AM`

A knock at the door.

Where am I?

I bolt upright.

"Can I come in? Just for a sec," he says.

It's Claudio! He knows I was out! I pull the covers up to my neck. "Yeah?"

He opens the door a crack and leans in. He's wearing a gray cardigan over a buttoned-up pink dress shirt. "It's Sunday morning," he says. "We're going to church."

"We are?"

"You and me. Church for people in recovery. You got fifteen minutes."

I have no choice. The guy owns me.

In the steaming shower, I wash party smells out of my hair. Wash Gary Jr. out of my life. Wash Maya away. Wash the person I was last night away.

Breathe.

Breathe in the steam.

I do it.

I inhale deep.

I exhale slow and long, letting tears and snot and memories and hopes wash down the drain in soap and water. And I tell myself I have a whole life ahead of me. Nothing that came before this moment matters. Not Friday night or yesterday morning or last night.

It doesn't matter where I've been the last year and a half. Or the years that led up to me being there. Or the years before those years. Because today is a new day. A day full of possibilities for a great life. And I'm starting this new day, this new life, by going to church.

When We Knew What Was Stupid

So then, just after spring break, Gary called.
He asked if we could talk before I met up with Maya.

Hands stuffed in pockets, inhaling wet salt air,
we stood at the end of the pier.
Gary's eyes followed the slow path of a cargo ship
as it made its way north up the sound, toward the strait.
No stops before open ocean.

 You know, he said, I been staying at Vaughn's.
 But his old Oma Ana is cold. She's kicking me out.
 So I'm moving on. To Portland.
 Where the indie scene is thriving.

He listed the things he needed in order for the move to happen.

 First and last month's rent.
 Repairs on the mini truck—breaks, tires, alternator.
 Money for utilities. Money for food. Money for weed.
 Money, he said. Money is what I need.

Money? I never saw a cent from my dad.
And he wouldn't even shop to fill the fridge.
My belly howling, I'd go to Grace for doughnuts
or show up at school just to beg in the lunchroom.

I told Gary I wished I could be of assistance.
But I had no access to cash. So I couldn't.

His eyes lit up. He insisted I stop the wishing,
and he made a list of all the ways I could assist him.

Get to know:

the times Lance Cushman comes and goes,
the times your dad is there,
how long he stays,
and the exact spot where they stash the cash.

And, Tonio, he said, when your dad is drunk and nodded off,
pocket the keys and make a copy.

That's it, he said. That's the list.
Do the research. Get the details we need.
Then sit back, relax, don't worry about a thing.
Cuz me and Vaughn, we'll do the deed,
then the three of us will all meet up,
and we'll count and split the proceeds.

I told him no. I told him the whole idea was stupid.
And the stupidest part? Including that kid Vaughn.

What is stupid, Gary said, is your dad deals drugs.
What is stupid, Gary said, is your dad and Lance
 bank money off addicts.
What is stupid, Gary said, is your dad is drunk all the time.
What is stupid, Gary said, is your dad doesn't buy you food.
What is stupid, Gary said, is your dad hit your mom
 till she had to move out.
And now that she's gone? He hits you.

He doesn't, I said.

What is stupid, Gary said, is you sticking up for your dad.

You don't have to decide right now, he said.
Go with Maya. Drink and be merry.
And we'll talk it over tomorrow.

As I walked away, he repeated the stupid scheme.
Like saying it again would convince me.

Just do the research, he said.
Just copy the keys.
And don't worry, Tonio!
Cuz me and old Vaughn...
we'll have it all under control.

SUNDAY `8:50 AM`

We're headed south on I-5 on the way to Tacoma. It's quiet in the car. I'm taking in Claudio's aftershave. His hair gel. Deodorant. He's a rainbow of man smells.

I watch towering evergreen trees and billboards fly by. "So, is this field trip just for me?"

"Nope."

I point at him.

"I go to Recovery Church every Sunday," he says.

I have misread Claudio. I ask him how long he's been sober.

He lifts his arm, revealing a wrist wrapped in rubber bands. "One for each year."

"What was your..."

"What was my *what*?"

I wave him off like it's none of my business.

"My drug of choice?"

"Yeah."

"I got in a car wreck my sophomore year of college. They

prescribed Vicodin for back pain. My brain decided it was helpful for other kinds of pain. I kept asking for more. My doc just kept filling prescriptions. When he stopped, I turned to stealing from medicine cabinets of friends and family. Before I knew it, I had worked my way up to a heroin addiction."

"Are you in a twelve-step?"

"Used to be. Now my program is church, and volunteering at this place called Haven."

"What's that?"

"A day shelter for opioid addicts. Same block as St. Catherine's. We feed people. There's a needle exchange. We'll administer Narcan if a client is overdosing. We funnel people toward social work, housing, treatment. Try to keep them alive as long as we can until support kicks in."

"That's cool."

He looks over at me. "You doing okay?"

I nod.

"Good. Sorry about getting on your case for sneaking out."

"It's okay."

"When I signed up with your mom, I signed up for all of it. All of her stuff. She signed up for mine. She helps me deal with my old mom. I want to do whatever I can for you. *Anything.* Just ask. But that doesn't mean I'm not going to say something when you cross a line."

"That's fair."

We pass the exits for Federal Way, then it's nothing but tree-lined freeway till Fife and Tacoma.

Claudio asks me if it's hard being out of Zephyr.

That question might seem weird to someone who was never inside. It doesn't seem weird to me.

"I have an idea what you're going through," he says. "When you're locked up, all you think about is how much better everything will be when you're out. Then you get out and life is still life. Your problems don't disappear just because you did time. And you're not free in the way you imagined you'd be."

I get queasy. Short of breath. I'm up in my head. Seeing the pictures. I'm banging on Maya's car. I'm on the phone with my dad. I'm wanting. I'm hating. I'm watching my mom tell me what I can and can't do. And resenting it.

I shake my head. I have to try harder.

"Don't beat yourself up. Just point your nose in the right direction and keep moving. Keep trying. Failing. Trying again. The world isn't going anywhere. You'll grow. You'll catch up. You'll figure it out."

"Uh-huh," I say.

"Uh-huh what?"

"I'll figure it out."

"You will," he says.

"I will," I say.

We're standing in the wet and cold outside a crumbling storefront in Tacoma's warehouse district. The folks we're with look nothing like churchgoers. There's a dude in a trench coat. A couple in matching leather jackets and matching big hair. A lady in a business suit. One in a fancy REI coat and hiking pants and sporty shoes. Some younger people in black hoodies. Jeans. A skinny guy shivering in a T-shirt and cutoffs. They share nods, smiles, handshakes, hugs.

Towering above them all is a giant, biker-looking dude with ripped muscles. He's wearing Doc Marten boots, black leather pants, and a matching vest over a bare chest. He's so pumped and friendly in the cold and wet, patting backs and greeting everyone.

We move inside to a big room that serves as the chapel. Nothing much on the walls. Nothing much at all except rows of white plastic chairs.

The big, bald dude takes the podium. "For those of you who don't know, I'm Pastor Spike. As God welcomes each and every one of his children into his kingdom, I welcome each and every one of you to Recovery Church." He asks that we welcome those sitting around us.

People say hello. They shake hands.

Pastor Spike closes his eyes. "I am on a journey, and I believe all who have come today, guided by Christ, are here to help me. And guided by Christ, I am here to help you."

As he opens his eyes, he catches mine. "You were brought here to help me," he says.

He points to Claudio and says, "He was brought here to help you."

That hits me in the gut.

"Everyone here," he says, "needs everyone else. Everyone is here *for* everyone else. And *that* is Recovery Church."

I see heads bobbing. Some eyes closed. Some smiles.

"It's a good day to be sober!" he booms. "Am I right?"

People shout, "Yeah, it is!"

"But my, oh my, aren't we a room chock-full of broken individuals."

People laugh sadly and mumble stuff.

"We are hurt. We are weak. We are addicts. We are messed-up sinners who have hurt those closest to us. And we are desperately in need of forgiveness." He gets quiet and says, "We need…" Louder now, he says, "No, we *really* need…" He laughs. The room laughs with him. He booms, "God Almighty do we really, really, really need forgiveness!"

There's an eruption of *amen*s and clapping.

I turn to Claudio. He scrunches his shoulders like, *Yeah, it's weird. Just go with it.*

154

"Now," Pastor Spike says, "it's our deep need for forgiveness that makes us *the most* capable of understanding how much others might need forgiving. Combine that profound understanding with our willingness to forgive, and that, my friends, is one heck of a superpower."

He says all it takes to spread understanding and forgiveness is making the decision to use your superpower. And that, when we forgive, we are doing the work that God sent Jesus to do. The work that Jesus tried to teach us to do.

"I have hurt others," he says. "I have hurt myself. And, my God, do I need forgiveness."

The congregation shouts, "You are forgiven!"

"Bless you, you beautiful people. I accept your forgiveness." He cups his ear to listen.

In one voice, a bunch of folks shout, "I need forgiveness!"

"You are forgiven!" Pastor Spike says.

Together, they shout back, "I accept your forgiveness!"

"Now, friends," Spike says, "it's time we engage in the practice of asking for—and accepting—forgiveness."

People get up and start doing the thing.

I scoot back in my seat, trying to disappear. But Claudio turns to me. "Antonio," he says, "I need forgiveness."

In those three words, I feel the pain of him hurting someone bad. I want to do whatever I can to make him feel better. So I say it. "I forgive you."

"I accept your forgiveness." He says it like I did something important. Then he moves away to someone else.

I stay right there, too freaked out to walk. I don't ask anyone for forgiveness, but I end up forgiving the business-suit lady. The cutoffs guy. And Pastor Spike.

As odd as this forgiveness practice looks, these people seem nice. Normal. Like my dad at the meeting yesterday. I wonder if they hurt their families as bad as he hurt me and my mom. I wonder if any of them did something so stupid, it meant they were taken away from people who needed them most.

Everyone moves back to their seats. I start walking to mine, but I get grabbed from behind by the wrist. The hand is dirty, long fingernails strong. It's attached to this ancient man with a grizzled face and bent back who smells like beer and old sweat and engine grease. I pull back—a reflex. He doesn't let go. He grips my shoulder tight with his other hand and stares right into me, his wide eyes desperate.

In a scratchy, weak voice, he says, "I need—I need—" He's breathing hard. Searching for the words. Bony fingers squeeze my shoulder and my wrist till they hurt. "I *need*—"

"You are forgiven." I say it quiet, feeling all eyes on me.

He shakes his head. His whole body shakes.

I'm shaking too because he doesn't let go. Like my words weren't enough or he didn't believe me. His eyes beg me to get real.

I want him to believe me. Because I want this to end. And cuz of how bad he needs it.

Louder, I say, "You are forgiven." Louder, I say, "It's okay. You're okay." *Louder,* "I forgive you." I practically shout it one last time. "You are forgiven!"

The man throws himself onto me. Hugging me, squeezing

me, kissing my cheek with his sandpaper face—like I'm the one actual living and breathing person he needed to be asking for forgiveness. The one person who needed to do the forgiving.

Claudio comes to help me out. He pats the old man's back and slowly peels him off me and walks him to his seat. But before the guy sits, he turns back to me, eyes watering, his palms and fingers pressed together, drumming praying hands from his lips to the space in front of his chest, thanking me, thanking me.

I catch some smiles and nods of recognition and appreciation as I take my seat.

Claudio elbows me and flashes a big smile.

I play that out in my mind, over and over. Pretty soon, I'm thinking about the days when I was reading comics, reading about superheroes all the time. I never thought how scary it might be to have so much power inside me.

When Hoping It Meant Something Big, I Worried That It Didn't

So then, after telling Gary I wouldn't do the research,
I wouldn't get the details, I wouldn't ever copy those keys,
I wouldn't help him and Vaughn rob Lance...

Gary and me parted ways.

I skipped to the second lamppost, hopped the rail,
climbed down, scrambled under,
bathed in the smells and sounds of this place
and the heavenly sunlight slicing through pier planks.

Maya sat, wrapped in the blanket,
back snug against the driftwood,
her freckled face framed by curls,
her lips smiling at the sight of me.

She lifted her eyebrows wickedly
as she revealed a half-full bottle of vodka.

Fijáte che.

Nice, I say.

And Junior? she asked.

Scoring weed, I lied.

Really, he'd gone off to talk to that Vaughn
about his plan to rip off Lance.

She smiled bigger, like happier,
cuz Gary Jr. being gone meant it would be just the two of us.

Suddenly, Maya's eyes got big.
Her arm shot out and she pointed at the water.

I immediately spotted it, a great blue heron,
perfectly framed by the pier above,
mud beach below, and pylons on the sides.

We each held our breath at the sight of that heron.
It stood statue still, stick legs sticking up from out of the sound,
its neck an impossible S,
its yellow sliver beak pointing south down the beach.

Watching Maya watch that bird, I snapped photos of her in my mind.

This Maya, this Maya...amazed by a bird, delighted by a bird,
thrilled by a bird, delighted by, thrilled by, life.

When people asked, I always said we were just friends,
but I'd been ready for a while to make that truth a lie.
And I believed it was the same for Maya.

After too short a time, beak pointed skyward,
wings slowly unfolding, unfurling,
downward pushing, upward lifting...

Maya's eyes brightened as she watched the heron
soar across the sky.

> ¡Bárbaro! she said with reverence.
> She does it to me every single time.

> I know, Maya.

> I know you know, Antonio.

She scooched closer, wrapping her arm around my back.
I squeezed closer, wrapping my arm around her back.

She twisted the cap off the bottle,
staring out at the bubbling sound like making a wish.
Then she sipped and savored and handed it over.

I held the bottle, feeling maybe I got drunk enough,
dizzy-giddy enough, just watching Maya.
Maya, delightedly mesmerized by that bird in flight.

You think it's the same heron every time? I asked.

Yes, she said. It is. And maybe she's here
to add more to this moment, to crystallize this night—
you and me here together—
into a memory that will last forever.

Maya took another sip.

I brushed the hair from her cheek.
She smirked, her eyes on me like she was wondering.

What? I said.

I dunno, she said.

Then she handed me the bottle and rested her head on my chest.
We watched the water just like that.
No words, as sky and sound turned black. And the rain came.

We folded the tarp over us to stop the drops from soaking us.
And we polished off the last of that vodka,
then started in on a bottle of rum,
passing it back and forth until, sometime in the night,
all the years of loving each other finally added up.

It was awkward at first,
figuring out where hands and lips were supposed to go,

so much blushing and giggling
till the situation got so far from awkward,
because her lips and my lips fit perfect, like they were made to,
like this was exactly how it was supposed to happen,
like this was how it was always meant to be.
It was the closest to the feeling of home I'd felt in the longest time.

But as we fell toward sleep, her smell and my smell
all mixed up in the cloud of booze wafting between us,
I wondered if we could have gotten so close, this close, sober.

I squeezed her tight. She sighed so sweet.

I opened my eyes. And the heron was back,
standing still at the edge of the water.
She looked at me, lifting her beak as if waiting for me.
So I closed my eyes and made my wish,
hoping someday me and Maya might kiss like this again,
with nothing between us but love.

I opened my eyes.

The heron's wings unfolded, unfurled, pushed down,
lifted her up, and away she flew once again.

On the way home from Recovery Church, we're flying up I-5 and I'm gazing out at Puget Sound's Commencement Bay. The barges, ferries, sailboats.

"Hey, man," Claudio says.

"Yeah?"

"Is your room okay?"

"It's good," I say.

"I just want you to know we're going to add on."

I was actually wondering if there was a plan. The house is two bedrooms and one bathroom. It was perfect for the three of them. And then I showed up.

"As soon as I get another union electrician gig, we can get our savings going again."

"Sure," I say.

"We want you and Olivia to have a comfortable space. So when you grow up and move away, you'll be able to come back whenever you want to or need to." He smiles. "Plus your mom wants a bigger bedroom with a bathroom."

I want to ask how they're going to afford that with my mom's massive hospital bill. I don't ask. "I'll help," I say. "I'll get a job."

"You concentrate on school," he says. "But maybe when you're up to it, I could teach you some electrical. Just something to get you by while you're figuring out what you really want to do."

I don't know why, but I ask him if he likes being an electrician.

"Sometimes I think I'm still figuring out what I want to be when I grow up."

We pass the Emerald Queen Casino and the last of the city.

"I liked making that studio for your mom," he says. "Putting all the pieces together."

"That's cool," I say. "And you're a great cook."

"Thanks. And I feel good when I'm at Haven. Sure, it's depressing. But when I'm there, I *always* feel like I'm giving it everything I have."

"You're helping people when you fix their fuses," I say.

"For sure. Haven's just a deeper kind of helping. Don't get me wrong, it usually feels like a losing battle. Sometimes people walk in the door in bad shape, and they look like the walking dead. Just *lost*."

The image of that guy's face flashes in my mind. The one from the first time I went to Lance's. The way he looked at me, like right through me.

"I remember how I was lost not so long ago. Now I'm winning their same battle. Maybe someday they'll be winning the battle. Maybe I'm a small piece of what makes that possible. That keeps me going back."

"How did you start winning the battle?"

"No magic. Just a lot of people doing the smallest things for me. Those small things added up. You can't carry anyone across the finish line. There is no finish line. But you can show people they're worth it. Haven did that for me when I was in bad shape. People treated me like I was worth showing up for. So I decided I was worth showing up for."

"It worked," I say.

"It's working," he says.

SUNDAY `12:10 PM`

Claudio and I are just a block from home when I spot it. A red Jeep parked on the street in front of the house. "Is that...?"

"Yeah," he says. "Tammy's Jeep."

"Probably just visiting?"

"I'm gonna check." He pulls the car over. Calls my mom. He nods as she speaks, his lips tightening, head slowly shaking, until he hangs up and turns to me, eyes on fire. "You promised me you wouldn't sneak out again."

"Tammy saw?"

"You screaming and banging on Maya's car last night."

My head drops into my hands. My fingers clench. My arm shoots out. I grab the door handle.

Claudio drives toward the house. "And that selfie before your meeting? Your mom thinks a blur in the background is your dad. That's just her worrying, right?"

Breathe, Antonio.

Oh no.

Breathe.

Oh hell.

Breathe! Breathe! Breathe!

I can't!

Claudio pulls into the driveway. "I'm walking in with you. We're gonna face the music."

We walk toward the house, Claudio's hand gripping my shoulder. "Chin up," he says. "We'll get through this. Stand tall."

We're halfway between the car and the house when a hand pulls the front window drapes open a crack. It's my mom bouncing a crying Olivia. She's staring right at me. But detached from me. Radiating rage and resentment. She threw this look at my dad a hundred times.

And once at me.

A look that said her life would be easier if...better if...

Claudio keeps walking. But I freeze in my tracks, looking right back at her. *I need you, Mamá. I need you.*

She rolls her eyes in disgust. Shakes her head.

I'm not him, Mamá.

I'm not him!

She turns her back to me. The drapes drop between us. And I'm cut off from her again.

Lost again. Alone again.

"It's gonna be okay, Antonio." His voice is a fading echo.

I worked so hard in Zephyr—*so hard*—thinking I could live a normal life. We could be a normal family. But that was fantasy.

What's real is, I'm still capable of turning my mom into a person who could turn her back on me.

I lift my arm and swat Claudio's hand away.

And I run.

When Waking Up Drunk, We Imagined a Future

So then, the morning after us kissing,
and me making a wish to a heron
that someday it might be different...

Maya and me woke with the rising tide,
unfolding, untangling legs from legs, arms from torsos.

She said her head ached.
I told her mine did too.
She said her breath stunk.
I told her mine did too.

She dug for the bottle of rum, gripped it, and shoved it my way.

    Try this.

It made sense that rum would help my breath,
cuz I was still a little drunk, and cuz Maya said it would.

I sipped, swished, swallowed, and handed back the bottle.

What we did last night, she said, we can do it again someday.

Kiss? I said.

Yes, she said.

Someday? I said.

Why rush, Antonio? We've known each other forever.
And we've got a chance to keep on saying that for the rest of
     our lives.
That's a long time. So slow is good.
It gives us something great to look forward to.

When is someday? I asked. Can you picture it? Circled on a
     calendar?

Nope, she said. But you can keep being nice to me.

I lifted the bottle, gulping without thinking.

Maya pulled it back, held it up, and said,

Someday will come sooner, the sooner we stop doing this.

Then she guzzled again.

Because this, she said, holding up the bottle, is bad.

We gotta go to school more! To sleep indoors,
in our own beds, in our own homes, more!
We need to start being the people we want to end up being.
Or we'll end up being the people we are right now.

As she said that, Maya pressed her palms into my cheeks.
She squeezed them, then kissed my lips again.

That was the last for now, Antonio Sullivan.

She held the bottle, shook it,
the splash at the bottom whirlpool-swirling.

And I knew what she was thinking: that we might as well finish it.

Then, good and drunk, we decided
this was the morning we'd start our lives anew.

Maya held the neck of the bottle. I gripped its body.
We ran to the edge of the water and tossed it in together.

And we said goodbye to a wasted teenage life.

Hand in hand, we marched up the hill to school,
Maya imagining the future the whole way.
She shared her dream of going to college
and of becoming a marine biologist.

To save our Sound.

I smiled, thinking, This is the real Maya.
Passionate. Caring. Driven.

You can do all that stuff, I said.

Someday, she said.

At Puget High's front doors, we hugged a fast one.

Consider yourself kissed, I said. Someday.

Someday, she said. Now you be good in there.

I'll be berry vood.

You just said berry vood.

No, what I said was, I'll be berry—I caught myself and tried it
*   again real slow.*
I'll be vvvvvverrrrrry gooooood, Mmmmaya Jooordan.

That's better! Now off you go.

I looked down the hall, measuring the long road that lay ahead.

Then began my journey toward a beautiful future...

One
slow
step
at
a
time
so
as
not
to
stumble.

SUNDAY `12:50 PM`

That look on my mom's face. It's like my legs reacted to it before I could, and they ran me all the way to this crescent-moon crack on the sidewalk. This place where I've waited a thousand times, knowing Maya's face would tell me I mattered, that she needed me and saw me for the best I was.

I turn to the house next door. Our old house. It's painted bright blue now. A new, yellow SUV in the driveway. Even some new bushes. Between half-closed curtains, I see a bald guy playing video games on a massive flat-screen. Nothing about our house is the same.

I toe that crack and look up at Maya's dolphin-pattern curtains. I laugh, remembering how she insisted they were *porpoises*.

This hasn't changed. This spot where we'd meet up, where we were good together. Where we can be good again.

I breathe in deep and let Maya fill my head. And I practice step nine. Apologies starting with last night. Starting with me going to Amanda's because I knew she might be there. Apologies for expecting her to give me more than what she told me she was ready to give. Apologies for banging on her car. For scaring her. Apologies for keeping her out nights when we were way too young for that. Apologies for not putting a stop to our drinking. Apologies for getting sent away and leaving her to put the pieces of her life together alone. And a pledge to be the opposite of all that moving forward. A plan for making amends.

I pull out my phone and thumb six little letters. Same as old times.

> I'm here

I wait for her curtains to flip back and reveal her face. Back in the day, she'd stick her tongue out or flip me off. Then laugh and disappear, only to spring out the front door and run right at me. A whirlwind hug and we were off to another adventure.

I don't get any of that. Just this text.

> Don't do this. Please, Antonio. Go.

Breathe, Antonio.
I inhale deep as I can.
I exhale slow as I can.
Good?
I'm okay.
You sure?
I'm sure. It's time to move on. I'm gonna live my life like I'm making amends to Maya, even if I can't say sorry face-to-face. I get my feet moving away from that crack, that window, those curtains. Because respecting Maya means leaving her alone.

174

Then again...I stop walking. To really think this through. Because maybe—I mean probably—it would help Maya's journey if she heard the words coming straight from my mouth. Straight from my heart. Cuz last night, she blamed herself for the bad stuff that happened to me. If she heard me taking responsibility for all that, I could take some of the blame and pain away from her. That would be my gift to her. That and wishing her the best on her path to becoming everything I know—*I know*—she is capable of becoming.

I walk up to her door. I stretch out my arm and a shaking finger. And I press the button.

In a second, there's a body in shadows, blurred behind a screen storm door. She steps closer and comes into focus. It's Rhonda. Blue sweat suit. Squinting eyes. Brown hair in a ponytail. She cracks the screen door and pokes her head out. "Sorry, Antonio, but you better go."

Rhonda has known my mom and me since I was a little kid. I tell her about Olivia.

"Maya mentioned that," she says. "Give Carmen our best."

"For sure," I say. "Maya says you're doing good?"

"We're fine, so..."

"May I please speak with her?"

She shakes her head. "Not a good idea."

"Literally for one minute."

"No, Antonio."

"Just to tell her I'm sorry. Cuz I blew it big-time."

"Yes, you did. Now go."

"Okay."

"All right," she says, waiting.

I take a step away. "Here I go."

"Goodbye." She steps back and lets the screen door slam. But instead of latching, it bounces open. I lunge forward and catch it, and before I can think it through, I got one arm and a leg inside the house, the screen door against my back.

Rhonda pushes the front door against me.

I push back—not pushing, really—just keeping it open, keeping it from slamming into me, which it would if I let go.

Rhonda puts her shoulder into it stronger, like I'm an intruder.

My ears tingle. My face gets hot.

"Stop, Antonio!" she says as she pushes and pushes.

"Okay," I say, "just ease up and let me get out, so you don't slam—"

She pushes even harder. "That's enough, Antonio!"

This is so stupid. I'm so stupid. But as long as I'm stuck here, I shout into the house, "Let me explain, Maya!"

"Jesus Christ," Rhonda says. *"Go!"*

I got my whole body into it so she can't crush me. "Talk to me, Maya! Please, Maya!"

A shout from upstairs. "No!"

Rhonda's jaw is grinding. Her face is beet red now.

"I'm gonna go," I say. I stop pushing. Rhonda doesn't, so the door slams me into the jamb. I squeeze my way outside, pleading. "I'm sorry, Rhonda. I'm so sorry."

She pulls the door fast. It slams. She stands there, staring at me through the screen. Desperate breaths. Sweat dripping down her cheeks. Fear and confusion on her twisted-up face. "What happened to you, Antonio?"

She stands there waiting for an answer. And like she's afraid of what I'll do next.

There is no next.

There is only Maya.

Rhonda closes the main door. She locks the locks.

I just stand there panting, gasping, empty, desperate, bent over and staring into that crack in the sidewalk, begging it to open up and swallow me.

I'm blocks away when I finally realize I'm running. No idea where I'm going. Just running and running down these stupid sidewalks with their stupid ghosts.

Until something inside pulls me and points the way. And I know exactly where I'm headed.

I should not go to him.

I don't even want to.

But I have to.

When I Tried So Hard to Be Good

So then, after making it
all
the
way
down
the
hall
without falling, I walked in late to Mr. Orton's math class.

He was pointing at the board, talking angles and degrees.

I walked so slow, about to try talking at the same time as walking.

    Helloooooo, Mmmister Ooor—

I didn't even finish his name,
cuz I tripped on a table leg and
dropped in a heap, right in front of Orton.

My God, the look on that man's face was classic!
Cracking up, I rolled onto my back.

The class erupted in laughter.
Orton couldn't get them back on track.
So he called the office to send someone
to come and take me away.

From Maya's house, it's about an hour walk down 19th, west on 223rd toward the water, then north up to Normandy Park, where the homes are bigger, with huge yards and tons of massive fir trees.

I double-check the address on a gray house on 6th Avenue SW. It's got huge windows in front, huge windows upstairs. There's a tall, skinny, curtained window to the right of the door.

Chin up. Back straight. Say why you're here. Get what you need. Then go.

The curtain pulls back a crack. It's him peeking out, eyes bulging at the sight of me. His face stretches into a smile, whitened teeth gleaming. He waves, and the curtain falls closed again.

The door opens. He's smiling. "What a surprise."

I stand tall. "I'm here to get my stuff."

My dad motions me to step inside, then stretches his neck outside fast, peeking one way and then the other before closing the door.

He leads me into a big, open room. To the left is the living room. It's got a yellowish shag carpet and sleek wood furniture. In the middle are a long dining room table and curvy wood chairs. On the right, orange appliances and dark-brown cupboards fill out the kitchen. Tall windows stretch the length of the room. The views are Puget Sound, Maury Island, and Vashon, with snow-capped Olympic Mountains looming in the distance.

My jaw just drops.

"I know," he says. "This was Nancy's parents' place. They died and left it to her a few years ago. We're planning to update it sometime."

I stare out at that view, not believing my dad actually lives here.

"Would you like a soda?" he says.

"Okay."

He pokes his head into the fridge. "Coke? Mountain Dew? Root beer? Dr. Pepper?"

Too many choices. I ask him to pick.

He hands me a can of Dew. "Have a seat."

I sit in a cushioned chair. He takes the sofa across from me. "Wow, Antonio," he says. "Honestly, there's a part of me that thought I'd never see you in this house."

I nod, no idea what to say.

"But here you are," he says. "That's good! Right?"

"Yes," I say. "But I can't—I need to—you know—"

"For sure, he says. I don't want to get you in—"

"Exactly. My stuff. Then I gotta go."

He hops to his feet. "Let's get to it, then!" He leads the way through the kitchen door into the garage, where there is a shiny red Miata, and a bunch of gardening stuff hanging from the pegs on the wall. Rakes, shovels, clippers. There are fishing poles too.

He points to a shelf at the wall in front of the car. "There are some boxes with your name on them. What are you looking for?"

"Um...my laptop...some clothes...some stuff from Abuelo Hector."

"Do you need to go school shopping?"

"I'm good."

"Does your mother know you're here?"

I shake my head.

"Let's get you home before we get in trouble."

"Right. Sweet Miata, by the way."

"Nancy's dad left her that. It's the original model. Hardly any miles." He opens the door. "Look at this." The leather seats are clean like it's never been driven, keys in the ignition all ready to go.

"Nancy hates it. She drives my Focus. She's out in it now."

He pulls down a cardboard box from the storage shelves. Sets it on the garage floor.

I pull back the flaps. On top are framed photos. One is the three of us dressed up for Christmas. I was in second grade, I think. My mom wanted a portrait, so we went to Penny's at Westfield mall. There's another one of me with Abuelo Hector from when I was in kindergarten. I'm gripping a spool of kite string, and he's got the kite. I think its Saltwater State Park. There's one of me and my dad at the Crypt. I'm holding an Iron Man comic, and he's got a Green Lantern. We're both reading, fake serious, totally posed.

I'm maybe seven or eight. I remember it. I remember us laughing as soon as the photo was taken. Makes me smile now.

"God," he says, "you and me at the Crypt. Those were the days. Do you mind if I—"

I hand it to him.

There's one of me and my mom holding up mugs at her booth at the farmers market. One of me and Hector eating fish-and-chips at Ivar's on the waterfront. We're looking across Elliot Bay to West Seattle.

Underneath the photos, there's a pair of jeans, a jacket, some T-shirts. My old Superman backpack is at the bottom of the box. I set aside the photos and my laptop. There's a backup phone battery and some clothes in the bag.

I dig for my Forlán jersey. I ask him if he's seen it.

"Geez, Antonio, I don't think so. Anything else?"

I squint and bite my lip, thinking there is something else. Something from him. I don't know what it is. But something is tugging at me.

I can see in his eyes he needs something too.

He smiles, red in his cheeks like he's embarrassed. But he doesn't turn away. "Are you all right, Antonio?"

I snap to. "I'm fine. But I better get—"

"Right!" he says.

I loosen the straps and slip the backpack over my shoulder. I take a step toward the door.

"Hey!" he says. "Can you wait? Just a sec? Be right back. I promise." He heads upstairs. I take the clothes out of the backpack and roll them up tight, trying to make more room.

He returns with a thick, sealed manila envelope. "I've been holding on to these ever since I closed the store." He hands me the package.

The message reads *Antonio, memories of us at the Crypt. You made those the best of times.* He dated it a couple months after I got locked up. About the time he lost the house and had to pack everything up.

He hands me a pair of scissors.

I cut a slit across the top, then reach in and pull out a stack of comics, each in a plastic sleeve. A few of our favorites from back then. The Falcon. The Silver Surfer. Squirrel Girl and the Great Lakes Avengers. Even an ancient Superman comic.

"You'll want to wrap them right back up. Store them in their sleeves and all that."

"Thanks," I say, locking eyes, not turning away.

He doesn't turn away either.

There's a tug in my gut, thinking about us back then. I want to say that. Like how great it felt every time he took me to work. The moment of being outside the door. The anticipation. Then he'd turn the key and open up. He'd have me flip on the lights, and it was magic when the heroes on the comic-book covers would pop to life.

My dad made that magic happen.

I see it in his eyes. He's thinking about it too.

I want to ask him what happened to him. But I just grip the envelope tight, knowing it's time to go. Before I do, I ask him about the fishing poles.

He snorts and says Nancy likes fishing.

"What about you?"

"You can't picture me out there? Sitting on a pier? Seagull crap and splinters? The smell of rotting fish?" He laughs. "I couldn't imagine it either. Till I tried it."

"You actually like it?"

"Boring as hell. But the boats drifting by...Maury Island. Vashon. The Olympics. I usually fall asleep at some point. And all the times we've gone out, I've never caught a fish. Doesn't matter. I love it. Me and Nancy will take you sometime."

I nod at that.

"We fly kites too." He says he keeps a big delta kite in the trunk so he's prepared if the wind picks up.

I tell him Nancy must be all right.

"She saved my life," he says.

I let that sink in. And think about the times I wished he were dead.

"She saved my life when I had decided it wasn't worth saving."

I don't see a villain now. I don't see a hero. I see my dad, who went through a horrible time. Made some terrible mistakes. And now he's doing better. My dad, the sober fisherman–kite flyer. "It's good you met her," I say. Then I thank him for my stuff and tell him I better go.

We head to the door. He grabs the door handle, but before he opens it, he says, "You know, Antonio, there's something I need to talk to you about."

"It's getting late."

"Real quick," he says.

"I have to go."

"It's important," he says, his face reddening, his hand gripped tight around the doorknob.

The garage door is shut. My dad stands between me and the button on the wall.

"Antonio," he says, "before, when I mentioned Lance calling me from prison? I didn't tell you why I brought him up."

"I have to go, Dad."

"He's out. Lance is. Out of prison."

"Okay, but I don't know what that has to do with—"

"He blames you, Antonio." It comes out like he's hating himself for this situation. "He blames me too. And he's coming after me for the money."

I think I could blast his hand off that knob. Bowl him over. Run past him and out of here.

Breathe, Antonio.

"I've got this new life thanks to Nancy."

I try to breathe deep. I just can't.

"But as supportive as she is, she will not understand me taking out a loan, or selling our cars, or needing to sell the house—whatever I'd have to do...." He searches me for an answer.

"For real," I say. "I gotta go."

"This new life I'm building. It's not just for me, Antonio. It's for *us*. To get us back to..." He looks down at the comics in my hand. Looks up, into my eyes. "Gary knows what happened to the money. And you've seen Gary."

"I haven't...seen Gary.... I don't know where he...I gotta go."

He laughs the saddest laugh. "I wish I'd never...Of all the

stupid things I've done…" He runs his hand through his hair like he's about to tear it out. "You know what the worst was?"

I tighten up inside as the images flood my mind.

"Making you deliver to Lance. That was cruel. Worse than… as bad as…because…oh God…" He starts crying.

I just stand there, nodding, frozen, stuck. My breath racing out of control.

"I put a tracker on your phone."

I take a step toward the door.

He leans his back against it. Through gasps and sniffles, he says, "I hope, someday, you can…" He shakes his head. "Can I get you another soda?"

"I'm going."

"Gary told you about the money. Otherwise, you'd just admit you saw him."

"I didn't—he didn't—that money is long gone by now."

"There was a lot of it, Antonio. Yet Gary is still living in that dump apartment. Still driving that rusted-out truck. The rest of the money is somewhere. He knows where. You know he knows. You're a good friend. You're protecting him. I respect that."

"I wish I could help you. I can't. I gotta—"

"When I mentioned the money to Gary, he started sweating and stammering. It makes sense. He was the last person who saw it."

"Maybe Vaughn—"

"Lance hired a guy to track Vaughn down. The guy got rough with him. All Vaughn would say is, *Gary Jr. knows*. The guy threatened Vaughn, saying he was coming back for him. After that, Vaughn disappeared. They finally tracked him down at his uncle's in San Diego."

"Did that guy go after Gary?"

My dad looks down at his feet.

"Did he?"

"Lance told me that was my job," he says.

"So you ran into Gary on purpose."

"He said you were his best friend and he couldn't wait to see you. Couldn't wait till you got out. I know you met him for doughnuts."

"What? How did you—? Right. My phone. Gary didn't mention the money. I swear."

"Antonio," he says, "I don't care that you lied to me about seeing Gary. Doesn't matter. I haven't earned your honesty. I'm trying to earn it now," he says. "We are in a situation here. With Lance Cushman. Who is violent. And who is coming after me for the money. He'll go after Gary. He'll sure as hell go after you."

"You followed me to the AA meeting," I say.

He wipes his eyes. "Everything I said there was true. Everything I've done to get better—it's all true. All real." He points to the comics. "That inscription is real. The future I want for us is real. If we can just..." He reaches out to touch my shoulder.

I flinch and jump back. My body remembers. I trip and fall to the floor.

"My God, Antonio." He reaches down to help me.

I scramble up to stand on my own.

"I wasn't myself. The stress. Life was too—I lost control. I'm in control now. I will never, ever hit you again, you hear me? I will never hurt you. Ever again. Never."

I nod.

"Do you believe me, Antonio?"

I nod.

"Are you sure?"

I nod.

He slowly lifts a hand, showing me his palm. He looks at it. Looks at me like, *See? It's all good. All safe.* He's asking me if it's all right.

I don't say no.

He reaches out.

I don't flinch.

He rests his hand on my shoulder. Grips it softly. He squeezes.

A jolt rips into me. Electricity shoots through my body. I wince but stand up to it.

He loosens his grip, eyes still on mine. Still wanting.

He sees it in me and finally lets go.

The electricity ricochets inside of me.

I shut my eyes tight to squeeze the feeling away.

An image pops into my head again. My mom holding Olivia behind the drapes. She's about to turn away. In my mind, I freeze time before the curtains drops. And I talk to her.

I'm making amends to you. I can because I'm not him. I'm coming back to you because I'm not him. I'm going to be there for you because I'm not him. Money's a stress. I'm going to relieve it because I'm not him. I'm going to prove to you that I am not him.

The picture fades out.

A picture of Maya fades in.

I am sorry. For everything. I'm making amends to you. I'm going to make things right. Money's a stress for you and your mom. I'm going to relieve it. I'm going to prove to you I'm not your dad. I'm not my dad. I'm not any of those men who showed up and turned your life upside down, then ran away and left you with nothing.

I open my eyes. He's there. His eyes bore into mine, waiting for me to say something.

"I'm going to see Gary," I say. "I'll figure out what's going on. Then I'll call you."

"When?"

"Later."

"Later when?"

"Tomorrow."

"Lance is coming here tomorrow. Make it tonight."

I don't know what to say. "Eleven?" It just comes out.

"Okay," he says. "Eleven. Just, uh...okay, yeah. Eleven works. Why eleven?"

Why eleven? "Cuz, uh, I'm seeing Gary at ten?"

"Are you asking me or telling me."

"Telling."

"Where?"

"We haven't decided yet. But...um...Westfield mall."

"Why Westfield mall?"

"Cuz he's working at, um, Cinnabon. Or is it Sbarro? I can't remem—"

"Doesn't matter. You're going to see him. That's good."

He reaches a hand out to my shoulder again.

I spring back.

"Oh God, Antonio." He pulls his hand to his chest. Closes his eyes. Takes a deep breath. Opens them again and says, "All right. We have a plan. When Lance calls, I'll tell him that you're getting back to me at eleven. But if you don't call at eleven, I won't have anything to tell him. And who knows what he might—"

"I'm going to ask Gary what happened to the money. I'm calling you at eleven."

"Good-good-good. Just..."

"Yeah?"

He looks at me like he's about to break in half.

"Yeah, Dad?"

"Keep your phone on you."

When, in Drunken Desperation, I Ran to My Mom

So then, just minutes after parting ways with Maya
at Puget High's front door...a minute after
tripping in Orton's class...

I sat, slumped, in Mr. Matthews's office,
head in my arms, leaning on his desk.

He cleared his throat. Asked me to sit up.

> It's good to see you in the building, Antonio.
> But not like this. What's going on?
> How can I help you? What do you need?

I sat up and lifted my chin to talk to him straight.
But my eyes got stuck on a framed photo.
Him and his whole family beaming love
in matching Hawaiian shirts
and leis around their necks.

> You guys went to Hawaii? I asked.

A few years ago, Matthews said. Maui.

I reached for the frame. Held it close to my nose and wondered.

Mr. Matthews pointed.

> *That's my wife, Suzette.*
> *My son Cameron, he's at Central, studying IT.*
> *He's graduating soon.*
> *My daughter, Janelle. She's headed to U-Dub on a soccer*
> *   scholarship.*
> *She wants to be a doctor.*
> *The youngest is my son William. He loves comics. He plays the*
> *   trumpet.*

I set the photo down and I ask Matthews about

> *Hawaii,*
> *other places he's traveled,*
> *where he met his wife,*
> *where they got married,*
> *how big his house is,*
> *if he ever did stupid stuff as a kid,*
> *and if he's made mistakes as a dad.*

Mr. Matthews answered all my questions
like they weren't stupid questions.

Then he said,

> *Antonio, we need you here. Every day.*
> *But we need you here sober.*

> *That's no problem, I said, because I'm never drinking,*
> *never getting drunk, again.*

> *The rules say I have to suspend you.*
> *Zero tolerance when it comes to alcohol.*

> *Please don't call my dad.*

> *But we're not going to suspend you without a plan.*

> *Please don't call my dad.*

> *We're going to set you up with some help.*

> *Great! Just don't call my dad!*

> *So when you come back, you'll be prepped for success.*
> *I'm bringing in Mrs. Lucrisia. And the social worker.*
> *And we'll start trying to get to the bottom of what's going on.*

> *That's fantastic, Mr. Matthews. It's great. Perfect. Awesome.*
> *Just, whatever you do, please, please,*
>   *please don't call my dad.*

How's your mom? Is she still living with her friend?

Yes.

Feeling better?

Yes, but it never lasts.

And your dad?

Same old. You know?

I do have to call them.

Don't, Mr. Matthews. Don't call them.

I know it's hard. But we have to get everyone on the same page in order for you to—

I am here, Mr. Matthews!
On board. Whatever you say.
Name it. I will do it.
Just
DO
NOT
CALL
MY
DAD!

Mr. Matthews's eyebrows lifted. Shoulders lifted.
Like nothing I said mattered and he was gonna call my dad.

I hopped to my feet and ran.

Out the office door, out the main entrance,
into the parking lot, south on 19th,
no stopping till Tammy's house.
Because after his call, I could never see my dad again.
I couldn't go home again.
I needed my mom.
I needed my mom.
I had to go live with my mom.

SUNDAY 2:25 PM

I run uphill in the drizzling rain to get out of Normandy Park. But the hill kicks my butt, and soon the best I can do is a brisk walk. By the time I finally make it into the heart of Des Moines, I'm soaked from head to toe as I look for a spot to dump my phone before I go to Gary's.

There's a branch of the King County Library on the corner. That'll work.

First, I head to the CVS across the street. The front door swings itself open.

No one's at the register. I make a beeline for office supplies. I pick up a silver Sharpie, then make my way to the front of the store.

Still no clerk at the register, but now there are two people in line.

I duck into the candy aisle. I look to my left. To my right. And slip the Sharpie into my pocket and walk on out.

I cross the street and walk into the library. I head for the bathroom. Tear the Sharpie out of its cardboard and plastic. I pull out my phone. I take off the cover. I write, *Property of Diego Forlán.* I snap the cover on, then head to the front desk and turn it in to the lost and found. And I walk out of there.

I went to see my dad.

I stole.

I ditched my phone. Murdock can't reach me.

Three terms gone in one hour.

If I make it through this day...

When She Would Not Take Me In

So then I stood at Tammy's front door,
panting from running all the way from school.
I took a sec to catch my breath,
reminding myself to stand up straight,
act polite, not drunk, not desperate.

I knocked nicely. Tak-tak-tak.

No answer.

I knocked harder. BAM-BAM-BAM!

No answer, so I shouted,

> Mom! Mamá! Mami! I know you're in there!
> I need to see you! I need to be with you!
> To live with you! Please, Mamá! Please!

I stumbled off the porch to peek in the window
but couldn't see because of curtains.
I stumbled back to the door, about to pound louder.

Then a squeak and tick as the mail slot lifted and Tammy said,

> You can't see your mom when you're like this.
> You know that, Antonio. You have to go.
> And come back later. But only if you're sober.

I understood why Tammy said that.
Cuz the last time I pounded on the door,
I pounded and pounded. I slapped at the windows.
I shouted so loud, reminding my mom I was the one who fed her,
kept a washcloth steaming hot or freezing cold for her.
I was the one who read to her, who prepped her needle,
who put on a brave face to poke her in the hip with meds.
I was the one who got between her and my dad.

I pounded and pounded and slapped and shouted all that.

And I left knowing it was cruel and stupid.

But there I was, back again,
pounding the door again,
slapping the window again.

It had to have looked and sounded bad,
but I was just so afraid of Matthews calling my dad.
I'd felt the sting of his wrath, time and again,
for so much less than being drunk in class.

I need you, Mamá!

I staggered back to slap the window again.
That's when I saw her standing there,
holding the curtain back with one hand.
Just enough for me to see tears streaming down her face.
She took a breath like she had no strength to take another.
She looked desperate, wanting, loving, hating,
losing, lost, gone.

I willed her eyes to meet mine.

When they finally did, I said,

> *Mamá, I can't go home.*

I said it like she would hear me through the window.

> *I can't go back, Mamá.*
> *I'm tired. I'm scared. I can't. Please.*

I slapped the window again.

> *¡¡¡PLEASE, MAMÁ!!!*

The look on her face said everything. The worst thing.

> *You are just like him.*

Her eyes fell. She turned away. The curtain fell.

My heart fell. Head fell. Knees weak, I fell.

The squeak-tick of the mail slot.

    I called the cops, Tammy said.

I stood up and punched my fist in the door.

    I'm not him!

And I ran and I ran. I'm not him. I'm not him. I'm not him.

SUNDAY

I'm dripping wet, knocking on the door at the Viking Glen Apartments.

"Tonio!" Gary says, phone in hand, beaming, smiling. "I was *not* expecting you!"

"I lost my phone, so I couldn't call first."

He raises his phone to his face and talks to the screen. "Sit tight. There's a lug I gotta hug." He lunges and squeezes me. "You could never stay away from Gary for long!"

I pat his back hard a couple times and pull away.

"You're a wreck," he says, shaking his head at me. "Just like old times."

"I walked from Normandy Park."

"What were you doing in Normandy Park?"

"Nothing."

"That's a long walk for nothing."

I know he won't drop it, so I tell him I was walking to get some space from my mom. "But let's focus on tonight," I say.

"You and your mom on the outs again," he says, trying to stop from smiling. "That means you are here...cuz you want your money...*and*...you need a place to stay."

"I don't think—"

"I need a place too! When my parents left for Nicaragua—"

"Nicaragua?"

"They're missionaries now. When they took off, they laid down five months' rent for me. Your timing is perfect because the fifth month was three months ago. I'm out of notices. And my parents won't answer my calls."

"Jesus, Gary."

"Not to worry. My cousin is moving in with her new Tinder boyfriend in Portugal. She swiped right cuz love at first sight."

"Where is this story—?"

"She needs to sublet her condo on Alki Beach. It's huge. Perfect for my film collective. Expensive as hell. Doesn't matter, because after tonight we will be flush with cash. So you can shack up with GJ in that bomb condo while you work it out with your mom."

There's a voice out of nowhere. "Uh, guys, I'm still here."

"Oh yeah!" Gary shoves his phone at my nose. "Say hi to your buddy."

Just like that, I'm face-to-face with those ridiculous bottomless-pit dimples, that most punchable face, that goddamn Vaughn. I stare daggers at him, wishing I could jump through the screen and wrap my fingers around his neck.

"Hi, Antonio," he says, lip quivering.

Gary juts his face between me and the phone. "The old crew

together again! And we're gonna fix past wrongs for Tonio! Right, Vonny?" Gary turns to me and mouths the words *Say something nice to Vaughn.*

I snatch the phone, power it off, and drop it on the sofa. "Tell me he's still in San Diego."

"Nope. Sea-Tac. At his Oma's house."

"Did he fly up because you told him what's going on?"

"I had no idea he was coming. He cold-called me a minute ago. Crazy coincidence, huh?"

It's not a coincidence. I close my eyes and try to catch my breath.

I can't. All I can think about is my dad telling me how desperate Lance is. He's in that room with Vaughn. I know it.

Nothing good will come of telling Gary. "Tell Vaughn we're changing plans," I say. "Tell him we're getting the money tomorrow."

"You mean lie to Vaughn?"

"Yes!"

"I have never lied to my bud. And I'm not starting now."

"The two of us can dig up the money, then cut Vaughn in later."

"I think you're forgetting something," he says. "I'm the only one who knows where the money is buried. So you and Vaughn are both at my tender mercy."

Gary powers the phone up. "Hey, pal," he says. "Bad connection. Where were we? Oh yeah." He shoves the phone at me again.

"Antonio," Vaughn says, tears streaming down his cheeks.

"I'm sorry." He wipes his snotty nose and admits he got greedy the day of the robbery. Then he got scared in juvie so he told his lawyer whatever he wanted to hear. "Those kids in there," he says, "were so mean. And the guards. My God. You should have seen 'em, Antonio!"

"I saw them, Vaughn."

"I wasn't trying to get you in trouble. I was trying to get my freedom."

"Forget it," I say.

"I can't forget it. I sold you out."

Gary punches me in the shoulder and whispers, "*Forgive Vaughn*."

"Don't forgive me," Vaughn says. "Cuz what does forgiveness mean if you do it because someone begged you?"

Vaughn wipes his tears and snot. "I am going to earn your forgiveness, Antonio. He turns his head like he's responding to someone hovering just off-screen. He nods at the person, then turns back to us, nervous. "That's just my Oma. She's trying to... pray. Can we get on with this?"

"Definitely," Gary says. Then he whispers into the phone. *"Tell me when you are clear of your Oma."*

Vaughn squints at us like trying to tap out a code. "She left. It's okay. Say whatever you need to say." He scrunches his eyebrows and twitches. "*No one* is listening."

Vaughn's attempts to signal us go right over Gary's head. "Men," he says, "we've waited so long. Finally, the day has come. We'll meet up at the Des Moines Marina Pier parking gate at two AM sharp. After we get there, I'll walk you to ground zero. And, Tonio, you are gonna appreciate the reveal."

"The reveal?"

"Ooh, I really wanna tell you guys where the money is. But I'm not. Cuz trust issues."

"Good," I say. "Don't tell us a thing. We don't need to know."

"Not falling for the reverse psychology, Tonio. As much as you love us and we love you, you have a very strong motive to screw us over. Especially Vaughn." Eyes on his screen, he says, "And you, my buddy, have a proven track record of being an unreliable hot mess. Am I right?"

"I'll own that," Vaughn says.

"That's okay, pal. Just means you got room to grow. Now, in regards to tonight, all you gentlemen gotta do is bring your muscles to the marina gate at two. Then leave the rest to me. Shovels, picks, bags for splitting the cash. I got all that stuff. We'll work fast, because Tonio has to stash his dough and make it to his meeting at school."

"I'll have the boat," Vaughn says.

"Oh my God, Vaughn!" Gary drops the phone and turns to me. "Vaughn being Vaughn. Just like old times." He puts on a fake smile as he lifts the phone to his face. "What was that, buddy?"

Sweat pours down Vaughn's forehead. "There's so much cash, Gary. Why be greedy?"

Gary gets his face into the screen. "What are you talking about?"

"Let's quit trying to pull one over on Antonio. We can split the money *three ways*, Gary, instead of two. We owe that to him, because it's our fault he got locked up."

I turn to Gary. "Were you really gonna—?"

"No! You always been included."

"Antonio," Vaughn says, "Gary said show up at two AM. The truth is, I was gonna be cruising him across Puget Sound in my twenty-foot Boston Whaler by one thirty."

"Oh my God!" Gary says. "There you go with the Boston Whaler crap again. I suppose you're gonna tell us *Magical Charlie* is gonna fly in on a jet pack?"

"I know it's hard," Vaughn says. "But we owe this to Antonio."

"Am I on a prank show right now?" Gary says, smiling wild. "This is a joke, right?"

"It's okay, Vaughn," I say. "I'm all ears."

"Remember how Gary used to talk about crabbing with Gary Sr. and his big brother off the north end of Vashon Island? Up by Dolphin Point. West of the ferry dock. That's where the money is—at the bottom of the sound in a metal box in a crab pot. We were never going to Rattlesnake. It was always our plan to cut you out."

"If it's true we were gonna cut Antonio out," Gary says, "why did we wait all this time to get the money? Why didn't we just get it back then?"

Vaughn's eyes go from side to side. He wipes his brow with the back of his hand. Takes a breath. "Because life got crazy with cops and courts and juvie. And I got sent away to California. And you were waiting for *me* to come back. That's why we waited. Now here I am. And that's why we're getting it now."

Gary gets in my ear. "Do not listen to Vaughn."

"I was woozy from crashing through that glass door," Vaughn

says, "so my memory is foggy. Plus, it was dark. So I don't know exactly where the crab pot is. Or what the buoy looks like. There are dozens of 'em up there. But Gary knows. He picked the buoy. His old man's buoy. Right Gary?"

"I'm gonna play the game," Gary says, winking big at me. "The money is in a metal box. In a crab pot. Off Vashon Island. At Dolphin Point. It's tied to my dad's buoy."

"You got it," Vaughn says. "I'll have my Boston Whaler gassed up and ready to go at the end of the pier at one thirty. Just exactly like we always planned."

"Sounds good, Vaughn," I say.

"Come on!" Gary says. "There's no way you have a Boston Whaler."

"Sure he does!" I say.

"It's because Charlie—"

"Oh my God, Vaughn! We all know *Charlie* is a figment of your childlike imagination."

"Doesn't matter, Gary. The important thing is, Antonio knows what's up with the money now, so you don't have to pretend anymore. See you guys tonight at one thirty."

"See you then!" I snatch the phone and shut it down.

"I don't get it," Gary says. "We don't need a boat."

"Of course we don't need a boat. Vaughn knows that."

"Then why is he talking about a boat? Why is he talking about a crab pot?"

"He's, um, playing like we're in *Ocean's Eleven* or something, right? Everyone on the team has a job. *He's the boat guy!* Even though there is no boat."

"And no Charlie," he says.

"Definitely no Charlie."

"And no crab pot."

"Did you really go crabbing up there back in the day?"

"Yup."

"Your dad's pots?"

"Nope. We partook of crabs from the pots of others."

"Of course you did." I march to the door. "See you tonight."

"At two?" he says. "Or one thirty?"

"Definitely one thirty."

Gary's eyes brighten. "Stay and de-stress with me, Tonio." He mimes lighting up a pipe.

"Can't do it. My parole terms."

"That's okay. Soon enough we'll be living the high life, lighting up all the sweet Kush we please, in the comfort of our very own condo."

"We'll see, Gary. Hey, it's just me and you now. You wanna tell me where you buried that money?"

"Like I said before, Tonio, I love you, but..."

"Trust issues. Got it."

Gary gazes up at me with big, sad eyes. "I'm worried, Tonio. It's all right if you don't shack up in that condo. But I'm afraid of what's going to happen to us after tonight. I can't take the idea we might be apart again. I just can't."

Oh God. The sincere love that pours out of this pathetic kid.

"We'll make it," I say. "We always do."

"You're right," he says, his smile growing. "That's the thing about us." He launches into me and squeezes tight. He pats my back and releases. "See you, Tonio."

"Goodbye, Gary."

I spring down the stairs, sprint across the Viking Glen parking lot, and head north on 30th toward the cutover to Pac Highway. I don't know if Vaughn's Boston Whaler is real. But I'm thinking it might be. I don't know if Charlie is real. But what is for sure real is, Gary's plan for tonight is shot to hell.

I feel short breaths racing ahead of me. I close my eyes and try to slow them, but I can't. Because of Gary Jr. And this time it's not because I want to punch him. It's because I just lied to him. I lied to the most loyal person I've ever met, about the most important thing in his life. Friendship.

Gary and me . . . we're not going to make it past this moment.

That goodbye was forever.

Because I have my own plan for tonight. And it doesn't include him.

It doesn't include Vaughn. Or Lance. Or my dad. Or whatever chaos is going to ensue after I'm long gone with that money.

SUNDAY `4:35 PM`

It's a different librarian than last time. He asks me to describe my phone.

"A Samsung J3. I'm pretty sure I wrote my name on the back. Take off the cover. It should say *Diego Forlán*."

He digs through a box. Finds it. Checks the back. Smiles and hands me the phone with a wink. "Good luck in the next World Cup, Diego."

He knows about Uruguayan soccer. I want to tell him my mom is from there. I want to tell him the days of Forlán's cannon shots off either foot are long gone. Now it's all Suárez, Edinson Cavani, and a bunch of up-and-comers.

But there's no time to chat. I walk out and check my phone.

There's a string of messages from my mom, begging me to come home, promising me we'll work things out, telling me how much she loves me.

I wonder how the same person who looked at me the way she

did could write those messages. The same person who saw something in me she didn't like. Something horrible.

I don't like that thing either. Words can't fix that thing. Talking isn't going to win her trust. Or Maya's. My actions have to do the talking now.

There's another text. This one's from Murdock.

C u in the morn. 7 sharp!

> Sorry so slow getting back @ u.
> Battery died. C u @ 7!

A cold wind whips through me. I shiver and look to the sky. Black clouds. There's going to be more rain coming. I pull my hoodie strings tight. And get my legs moving. To the marina this time.

Bzzt!

A new text.

Where r u?

It's Maya.

SUNDAY `4:45 PM`

Maya squeals her Civic into the library lot, swerves into the book-drop-off lane, and slams her breaks. I see it in a flash of her eyes. She's boiling.

I walk fast to the passenger side. She hits the locks and rolls the window down a tiny crack. "If you're expecting some kind of fairy-tale news, you're out of luck. Okay?"

I nod.

"Can you be both disappointed and calm?"

"Yes."

"And you can be nice to me?"

"Yes."

"Like my old best friend? And not some random jerk?"

"Yes. I can. I promise."

She unlocks the door and tells me to get in.

I got this need to start apologizing. But I can't catch my breath. I just get in the car. I press my back into the seat, close my eyes, and try to inhale.

But my breath catches in my throat as Maya stomps on the gas and we rocket out of there.

• • •

She whips into a spot in the Angle Lake parking lot and slams the brakes. She jumps out. I get out too and watch as she pulls a duffel from the trunk and slams the lid. She marches fast down the path lined thick and dark with ferns and evergreens, all the way to this hidden lake off Pac Highway in the heart of Airportlandia. This lake that always made me feel so far away from everything. And so close to Maya.

We end up at the massive log at the far end of the grass beach. *Our spot.* We drop our packs and sit, backs against that log like we've done a thousand times.

She leans forward and turns to me, like she's ready to explode. Then she puts a hand up, stopping herself. She closes her eyes. Shakes her head slow. Takes in a deep breath. Leans back again.

We watch clouds for the longest time.

I start searching the trees.

Scanning the water.

Hoping our heron will make an appearance. Hoping Maya spots a bald eagle. Or that one of the river otters shows up. Or that some other miracle of nature will get us looking in the same direction, lighting up our eyes, allowing us to share a magical wish-worthy moment. Like old times.

No luck.

Eventually, she lets out a calm sigh. "Damn, Antonio," she says. "It's actually nice being back here."

I nod because it's smarter to not talk right now.

Then I talk, because I'm not that smart. "At Zephyr I dreamed about being together again. Here. At Saltwater State Park. At the marina. Just us."

Eyes on the clouds, Maya's jaw locks. Her cheek twitches.

"I understand things are different," I say. "It's just hard imagining my life without you."

"I know," she says.

"I guess that's why I seem—"

"Desperate?" she says.

"Um."

"Out of control?"

"Okay."

"Violent?"

"Come on, Maya."

"You were never like that before."

I tell her it was stupid fighting over the door with her mom.

"And at Amanda's? What was that?"

"I don't know."

"Antonio," she says, voice trembling, "should I be afraid of you?"

"Damn, Maya, you know I would never—"

"Hurt me?" she says.

"I wouldn't," I say. "I couldn't."

The look on her face says she's not so sure.

"I'm sorry. I am so, so sorry."

"It's not about *sorry*. It's about are you gonna be a safe person when life gets difficult? Or are you gonna be like your dad?"

"Jesus Christ, Maya! No!"

"Maybe he taught you some stuff you should never have learned."

I turn away. Lean back. Focus on clouds. And I try so hard to breathe.

"Get help, Antonio. Talk it out with somebody just in case."

I nod and nod as a breath catches in my throat. I gasp for air and I can't stop the tears.

"I know you started building up expectations ever since we kissed at the pier that night." She reaches over and wipes my cheek with a finger. "And you thought we would pick up right where we left off."

I nod, sniffling, snotting.

"Then I shot you down hard and fast. This idea of us in your mind, it went from being everything to nothing."

More nodding and snot.

"I could have found a better way to break it to you," she says.

"Was that the whole plan?" I say. "For us to be nothing?"

Eyes on the water, Maya shoves her hands in her pockets. "After I got sober, I realized I didn't know how much of us kissing was us loving each other, like so deep it would be worth all the work it would take for people like us to be together and stay together…and how much of us kissing was us being lost and wasted and desperate."

"It wasn't any of that, Maya."

"That was a hard time. It got worse after you went away. I'm getting better. But I still don't know what I want. From other people. From myself. I'm still trying to figure it out."

I don't know what I want either. Besides Maya. I laugh. Quiet. Sad. Defeated. "I wanted to do step nine. I thought that would get us somewhere fast. I was stupid."

"Look at me," she says.

I look her right in the eyes.

"If it wasn't for me, you never would have gone to school drunk."

"What are you talking about? I was the one who—"

"Shut up!" she says. "I tried step nine at Amanda's. You shut me down. Why?" She stares at me with big eyes, taking my heart into hers.

I get this feeling, like a tapping at my shoulder, something I been brushing away forever.

Maya is making me face up to it. To see it. To feel it.

I close my eyes and inhale deep.

I exhale slow and travel into a dark corner of my mind. I reach out for the thought, and when I've got it, I start crying again because I don't want it inside me anymore.

"Okay," I say, wiping my eyes. "You always brought the alcohol. I never needed it, Maya. I never wanted it. But I needed *you*. I wanted *you*. I always wondered who we'd be without alcohol. But I was too afraid to ask for that. Because maybe I'd find out you didn't want me."

"I know," she says.

"I get it. Life is hard. People do stuff to deal. And people have stuff that, when they start doing it, they can't stop, and there are other people that get mixed up in that. I know you were just doing the best you could to survive. But still, this part of me—this little part I'd shove down every time it got close to the surface—blamed you for the mess I got into."

She's still looking right at me. So calm. So open to me.

I say it again. "I blamed you."

She nods.

"I'm doing something with that blame now. I'm letting it go. I'm forgiving you."

I don't look at her. But I hear her breathing deeply now.

"You need to let it go too," I say.

Maya looks up at the sky. She wipes her tears. "I hated feeling like I had to convince you to drink all the time. I thought you were weak for letting me. I'm sorry."

She pops up, grabs a big stick, runs at the water, and lets it fly. She waits till it splashes, then turns and shouts back at me. "I'm forgiving me," she says, walking toward me again. "I'm forgiving you too, Antonio. For last night. For today. And for all those years of being my codependent copilot. I'm letting it all go. Every single thing."

"That's good," I say.

"But I'm not all the way there in my program, in my life. And if we have any shot at being healthy together someday...*friends someday*...we have to get healthy apart."

"How do we know when...?"

She shrugs her shoulders. Smiles. "When we like ourselves, maybe? Or mostly like ourselves? Maybe then?"

"You don't like yourself?"

"You do?"

"*Come on*, Maya."

"You know what?" she says. "I'm getting there."

"Good. There's a lot to like."

She sits up taller. "I'm a senior, Antonio! Can you believe that?"

"How did it happen?"

"Mrs. Lucrisia put me on a catch-up schedule. I'm doing independent study from home. Some online classes. I go to school and check in with her, and I have an in-person meetup in Burien with my online teacher once a week. I've even taken some classes at Highline College. I'm not quite going to make June graduation at Puget. But if I pass my classes this spring, I just have to take history online and a chemistry class at Highline this summer and I'll graduate in August."

"Congratulations, Maya."

"Thanks."

"What do you want to do after?"

She shrugs.

"What's your wildest dream?"

She says she's not thinking past tomorrow.

I tell her there must be something.

She wraps her arms around her knees and pulls them in tight. "There's a research vessel in the marine biology department at U-Dub. You have to distinguish yourself to get on it as an undergrad. You can get on for sure if you're a grad student. One way or another, I want on that boat someday. I want to sail to the Galápagos. To Antarctica. I want to study our orca pods. I want to let the world know what we're doing to these animals, what we're doing to ourselves."

"Go for it," I say.

She laughs a tired laugh. "I will. But for now, getting to my dreams means setting them aside and dealing with reality, and doing the next right thing today." That's when Maya reaches into her bag and starts pulling stuff out.

There's a beaded bracelet I made her in middle school art. A perfect moon-snail shell I found at Saltwater State Park. A key to our old house. A seal plush toy from when we were still in elementary school. It's a punch in the gut.

"You really need to give this stuff back?"

"It's hard to let you go, Antonio."

The way she's throwing stuff at me, I'm not so sure.

As long as she's at it, I ask her if she has my Forlán jersey.

She thinks about it, then says she remembers wearing it that last night together under the pier. But she gave it back in the morning and I wore it to school. She remembers me stumbling down the hall in it.

She zips the empty duffel shut. "That's all there is," she says.

I put everything in my backpack, then turn to face her. "I'm going to show you, Maya Jordan. I'm going to live right and show you."

Maya's brown eyes get bright, her smile wide. "Go for it, Antonio," she says, so much love in her voice. "Seriously. But don't do it for me. Do it for yourself."

I get it. But the idea of doing great only for me feels so damn lonely.

She grabs the empty duffel bag. "You going to school tomorrow?"

I tell her about my transition meeting with Officer Murdock and Mrs. Lucrisia in the morning. I tell her it's a term of my parole.

"Wow," she says. "Get there on time, Antonio."

"I will."

"Hey, what's going on with you and Gary Jr.? You two okay?"

"We're good," I say, a twinge in my gut.

We walk side by side to the parking lot. She asks me where I'm headed next.

I tell her maybe I'll walk to the marina. I know she thinks I'm going to drown my sorrows in our memories. She's half-right.

"That's far," Maya says. "You sure you don't want a ride?"

I tell her yeah even though I'm sure I *do* want a ride. But Maya can't know what's really going on at the pier. "So, um, I'm just gonna..." I step away like showing her I'm walking.

"Hey," she says, stopping me. "Bring it in." She holds her arms out.

I hold mine out. And we slowly make a hug happen. She tightens her squeeze and holds on. And I exhale something deep I didn't know was still inside me.

Too quick, Maya flashes me a sad smile, turns away, and springs toward her car. She gets in, yanks the door shut, backs up fast, and motors toward Pac Highway. I watch her Civic stop at the park entrance. Her left signal flashes. Traffic clears. She makes the turn. And she's gone. No looking back.

Tears and rain start falling. I close my eyes and wish as hard as I can that when I open them, Maya will be driving right back into the lot.

Doesn't happen.

As I cry my way toward Pac Highway and onto the Des Moines Creek Trail, I admit to myself that dropping a bunch of money on Maya and her mom would come off as a desperate attempt to pump life back into *Antonio and Maya*.

Goodbye can't come with a catch. Neither can forgiveness. As much as I want to beg, to fight, to try...there is only one thing I can do for Maya Jordan. And that is *nothing*.

I try to breathe deep to stop crying. I can't. My lungs ache. My guts ache. Saying goodbye to Maya aches.

But saying goodbye to wanting so much? Goodbye to un-realistic expectations? Goodbye to desperation? Goodbye to making someone feel like they could never give you enough of them? All that stuff has been inside me forever, sitting right on top of dreams of Maya, hopes for Maya, fantasies of Maya. *Wanting*. It filled me up. It propped me up. And now it's gone. And the ache is my body fighting to keep upright, fighting to keep from imploding into the empty space that's been left behind.

The trail is tree-lined, mossy, dark and getting darker. I pick up the pace. I have a long night ahead of me. And a lot to figure out if I'm going to end up with that money and erase six digits' worth of medical bills and make that dream house happen for my mom and Olivia and Claudio.

That's what's propping me up now. The idea that their lives can be made better. And I'm the one who's going to make it happen.

When I Thought There Was No One Else

So then I ran toward home, from Tammy's place,
trying to shake that look on my mom's face.

But it didn't matter.
It was just another mental image I couldn't erase.

At the house, I peeked inside,
and, thank God, my dad was sleeping.

I turned the key, slowly.
Nudged the door, creaking. And I snuck my way in, creeping.

I grabbed my dad's key ring,
took spare change, and loaded my backpack with clothes.

I took his Focus
to make copies of Lance's keys at our local Home Depot.

Back home,
I replaced the green ring and busted fast out of there.

Cuz Matthews's call
was coming soon, and I couldn't be anywhere near.

I pointed myself
toward Gary's place and called him up on the phone.

I said, I'm in.
Notify Vaughn. I did my part, now you're on.

Gary asked
how long I'd be. I told him, Thirty flat.

He wouldn't shut up
about how much he loved me. He went on and on like that.

SUNDAY `6:30 PM`

Dripping wet from the nonstop drizzle, shoes and socks sloshing with every step, I walk the length of the pier all the way to the rail. I scan the marina and the beach. Seagulls cawing. Waves lapping. Those smells. Salt. Seaweed. Salmon grilling on a yacht.

The sun will start dropping soon. Dark and cold are coming. More rain is on the way.

On the marina side, south of the pier, a hundred moored white boats bob in the choppy water. Mud, rock, and barnacle-covered oyster shells blanket the beach on the north side.

Where did Gary Jr. and Vaughn bury that money? If they dug the hole close to the waterline during low tide, they would have needed to bury it deep. Otherwise, in time, tides would have dug up the money and carried it away.

But that night, the clock was ticking. They had to dump the money fast. Plus, Vaughn's head was messed up. They couldn't have dug down that far. So the bags had to be buried up on the back beach, where the water would only reach during the year's highest tides.

Gary Jr. said I'd appreciate the reveal. There's no reveal for me to appreciate without the spot being attached to a shared memory. All our memories—most of them, anyway—are connected to our hideaway under the pier.

I run back toward the parking lot, all the way to the second lamppost. I hop the rail. Climb down a few feet. Then let go and land in the mud and muck and rock. I scramble under and up the back beach until I'm standing, hunched, at the foot of the driftwood pile.

There are two huge dry bags buried in that pile. We kept an old brown sleeping bag, a blue tarp, blankets, extra sweatshirts, in those bags. For a while we kept newspaper, matches, and some dry kindling in there too.

I lift some limbs and spot a moldy, wet Seahawks blanket wrapped around a limb. I find a sweatshirt. I move bigger limbs and stumps and find the blue tarp. Then it's nothing but massive logs Gary and Vaughn never would have had the time or strength to move.

The dry bags are gone.

I lie down, my back against a log for the second time today. My butt sinks into the cold, smelly mud. A big shiver, then tingles all over, warmth in my chest, my belly. My jaw loosens, then opens wide into the biggest yawn.

The wind whips off the sound, directing the wet and cold right at me. I pull my hoodie strings tight again. I close my eyes and play that night over in my mind.

Gary and Vaughn scrambling under the pier in the darkness. They're hauling shovels and bulging plastic bags full of money. Shoving those plastic bags into the nylon dry bags. And rushing to bury them in a place where Gary could easily find them when the time was right.

I open my eyes to scan the beach once more. There has to be something marking the spot. But I have no idea what it could be, no idea where the money is buried.

A yawn hits me like a tidal wave. My eyelids are so heavy. I let them close for just a second. It feels so warm. Another yawn. I force my eyes open again. Then close them one more time. Just for a second.

Someone pokes my shoulder. I knock the hand away.

"Wake up, sleepyhead."

I tell myself it's a dream. And in that dream, I'm taking in the scent of hamburgers. *Pete's Burgers.* My stomach growls.

"Hope you like bacon, cheese, and grilled onions."

I wipe my crusty eyes. Claudio comes into focus. He's standing there in boots, an oversize yellow raincoat, and a wool fisherman's cap.

"What's up?" he says, smiling big, taking a seat, and handing me the wrapped burger.

The heat through the waxy paper warms my fingers. I unwrap it and dig in.

Claudio unwraps his and takes a bite. "That vato at Pete's, man. Rafael. He's been manning that grill, killing these burgers, for what, twenty years?" Claudio hands me a Red Bull. "There's fries in the bag," he says, gazing out on the sound, toward the forest islands, Maury and Vashon. He's not asking anything of me. So we just sit in this moment of Pete's and beach.

But soon enough, burgers and fries are gone, and there are two empty Red Bull cans. Claudio reaches for the wrappers. He stuffs them and the cans into the paper bag and says, "All right, then." He juts a thumb in the air. "Heading out." And he walks, crouching so he doesn't bang his head on the planks above.

"That's it?" I say.

"What's it?" he says, stopping and turning to me.

"Oh. Um. Nothing. And, uh...thanks for the burger? And see you later?"

"Antonio, your mom wanted me to see if you were okay. You look okay enough, so—"

"Maya told her where I was?"

"Your mom freaked out about you running off. You didn't return her texts, so she called, and Maya said you might be here."

"And my mom sent you."

"Yup."

"If she really wanted to know how I was, why didn't she come?"

Claudio tilts his head to one side. "Um, Olivia. And this spot you've chosen is dark and wet and cold and muddy. And mixed up in that mud is seagull crap and rotting seaweed and rotting fish. It's miserable down here, Antonio."

"So you're just taking off? No lecture?"

He smiles at the word. Then a thought fades that smile away. "Back in my worst times, no *words of wisdom* from an authority figure were gonna stop me from doing the stuff I was gonna do. I got pissed at people for even trying. It had to be my decision to talk. Until then, it didn't matter what anyone said, so..."

I nod.

"You know what did matter?" he says.

I shrug my shoulders.

"Getting fed."

"I'm sorry I ran."

"Are you?"

"I don't know if I can live with my mom." My heart and breath race again.

Claudio bites his bottom lip, nods, and presses a hand against the pier boards above, like he's perfectly content to be crouching there, waiting for an explanation that might not come.

I try to do my breathing. I can't. My tears flow.

He sits back down and fishes a napkin out of the Pete's bag.

I blow my nose and tell him I saw my mom standing at the window holding Olivia. "You know that look people throw at you when you're too much for them to handle?"

"I'm familiar with it."

"Someone who is supposed to love you, looking at you like their life would be easier if you weren't in it. And you know it's true. And you think *you* might be better off without you."

The look on his face says he's remembering times.

"As much as you hate them in that moment," I say, "you still love them. You don't want them to feel angry or scared because of anything. But especially because of you. So you run."

I wait for Claudio to explain how wrong I am about my mom. He doesn't. He just asks me what I'm going to do.

I don't tell him how bad I want to go right back home with

him. Or how bad I want to fix things between me and my mom. Or how tonight I'm trying to make her life—*and his*—easier.

I look at Claudio and imagine him at his worst. In my mind, I see that strung-out guy the first time I delivered to Lance's. But with Claudio's eyes. The guy's pockmarked, sunken face is Claudio's face.

"What was it like?" I ask him.

"What was *what* like?"

"Before you got sober."

"Happy to share my story," he says. "Not sure it's on topic."

"It is."

"All right," Claudio says. "I can do that." He tells me about the excruciating back pain he felt after his accident. The relief that came with getting high. The pain and emptiness that followed when he came down from the high. The desperation to feel the high again. He got lost in that cycle.

He says it must have been horrible for his family—the things he put them through and what it must have been like for them to watch him destroy himself. He talks about how hard some of them tried to help and how some of them didn't try at all.

He talks about people he works with at Haven. The people he tries to be there for, regardless of how messed up they are.

I tell him about the people I'd see at Lance's when I made deliveries. Opioid addicts. Zombie faces. "One of them could have been you."

"I was done with all that by the time—"

"You know what I mean."

"Yeah," Claudio says. "Could have been me." He reaches a hand to my shoulder. His palm. His fingers. He rests them there.

I swallow. Close my eyes. The feeling of his hand on my shoulder. Warmth radiating through his fingers into me.

"You didn't choose to do that," he says.

"I could have chosen *not to*."

"Nope. That stuff isn't on you," Claudio says. "It's on your dad."

"It *was* me."

"You were a kid. You were trapped. You were afraid."

"My dad is tracking my phone."

Claudio's jaw drops. His eyebrows scrunch. "So that *was* him in that selfie."

"I didn't know that when I took it."

"You have to call your PO."

"I can't," I say.

"I will," he says.

"My dad came to the meeting. I saw him walk in. I knew he was there. Calling Murdock will make everything worse."

"Make *what* worse?"

I look at him, pleading to him to stop asking questions.

Claudio closes his eyes. He's the one doing the deep breathing now.

In the silence, I scan the mud all the way to the end of the pier. I scan the pier planks above, desperately searching for an answer.

Right away I spot a memory. Black char on the underside of a pier plank. Just twenty feet from where I'm sitting. My mind is flooded with the images. *Ghosts.* Gary's bottle rocket on the Fourth of July. The pier burning. Me and Maya putting out the fire. *That damn bottle rocket. That damn knot. That black char mark, a reminder of how stupid we were.*

Claudio lets air out in a stream, opens his eyes, and says, "Okay, Antonio. Just tell me if you need anything."

"Tell my mom I'm fine."

"I will," he says.

"There's one more thing."

"What?"

"Are you driving Uber tonight?"

"Yeah."

"Take this." I hand him my phone. "Just for tonight."

"What? Why?"

"My dad."

"Oh. You don't want him to know where you are."

"I want him to think I'm not here."

Claudio looks at me like I'm a mystery. And like he knows me better than anyone. "There is something gnarly going on," he says.

I nod.

"And you are not going to tell me what that is."

"I can't."

"Try."

"It's just... Going away didn't fix everything. There's pressure."

"From your dad."

"And worse than him. But I can relieve it. I just need a few hours."

"What if you don't?"

I look up at him.

He sees it in my eyes. He nods. "This sucks, Antonio!"

234

"I know," I say. "I'm sorry. I am so sorry."

He pulls his phone out. "Not my Uber phone. My personal phone. In case of emergency. You call, and I'll come as fast as I can." He hands it over. "Do not make me regret this."

"I won't."

"I might finally meet your dad," he says. "Can't make any promises how I'll react."

"He doesn't know who you are. Play dumb. You were fishing at the pier. You put your phone down and picked mine up by mistake. Just give it to him. That'll work."

He looks at me for a long time. It's like he's asking me not to do this.

I look right back. Pleading with him.

"Antonio, if there are calls or texts from your mom, let me know right away. I'll tell her we mixed up phones when I saw you."

"Sounds good."

"And that phone is for calling and texting me or your mom. No one else."

"Got it."

"And I'm gonna need my phone back tonight. Before I see your mom at home."

"One thirty," I say. "Westernco Donut."

Claudio nods. "I'll be there." He turns and walks. I watch him go. When it's safe, I bust out of there. I know where Gary Jr. buried the money. I need supplies, and I know where to get them. But I have to kill time until it's all the way dark and the pier is closed.

I need to get dry. I need a hot cup of coffee. And a lemon-filled doughnut wouldn't hurt.

When I Finally Turned to Grace

So then... after setting up Gary and Vaughn to rob Lance...

I waited alone in our Westernco booth,
drumming the tabletop, staring at a lemon-filled,
squirming, nervous, imagining what could have gone wrong,
because Gary is Gary, and Vaughn is Vaughn,
and stealing is wrong, and so far in life, my luck has sucked.

Grace took the bench seat across from me.

> You look worried, she said. Should I be worried too?

I looked at Grace, the kindness on her face, all her hopes
   for me...

> I drank. I got suspended.
> My mom won't take me in. And I can't go back to my dad.

> Your life sounds difficult, Grace said.
> May I tell you a story?

Little Grace was a homeless orphan on the streets of New York City
when she set out on a solo cross-country adventure,
begging, borrowing, stealing, all the way to LA.
As a teen, she cleaned homes and offices.
Graduated high school, obtained a real-estate license.
Became a developer. Made one brilliant deal after another.
She built an empire while breaking the hearts
of so many weak, wealthy men.

I was ruthless. But I didn't only hurt them,
I hurt people who cared about me too.
But soon enough, I got what was coming.
Convicted of racketeering, I lost everything.

How did you end up here? I asked.

My story has too many twists and turns to recount now.
But that's life. You're up one day. Down the next.
The point is, what kind of person will you choose to be
when you choose to rise again?

And remember, Antonio, even though your
parents are far from the best, you have good friends!
And an old lady who sees the very best in you.

Who? I ask.

Me! she says.

Grace Cho offered me a deal I couldn't refuse.
A back-room futon. And a life in doughnuts.

I immediately accepted.

Then she went on talking. Accounts of Tommy and the mob,
their meeting in prison, witness protection...
The epic tale of Grace's life—it seemingly had no end.

SUNDAY 8:10 PM

The bell jingles and the door closes behind me as I head for our booth, rainwater dripping off me with each step.

"Well, well," Grace says from behind the counter. "Look what the cat dragged in."

"Nice to see you too, Grace."

As fast as I can take a seat, she's right there, tossing me a kitchen towel and setting two lemon-filled doughnuts on the table.

"Thanks," I say, drying off. "You got coffee?"

Grace slides into the seat opposite me. "Just brewed! Could you grab a cup for me too? You're so sweet."

I bring back two mugs and set them on the table. One black for me. One with two sugars and two packets of Equal for Grace.

"Something's off," she says. "It's the night before your first day back in school. You're soaked. Your clothes are dirty. You smell like an oyster bed. You're alone. And you are *here*."

"I'm on my way home. Just wanted to say hi."

"Hi back. What else you got?"

I take a deep breath to finally say what I need to say.

I'm too slow. Grace huffs, waving me off. She stands and bolts back to the counter, through the swinging door and into the kitchen.

I take a sip of coffee, tracking the heat as it travels down my throat and into my belly.

Back in a flash, Grace drops a paper bag on the table.

I reach inside and pull out a shirt. It's sky blue. *Celeste.* Number ten in black. Uruguay's official shield over the heart. And the name across the back, *Forlán.*

"I been looking for this."

I head to the back bathroom. Take off my wet hoodie and T-shirt and slip the jersey on. I check my reflection in the mirror. I fill it out good. I grew when I was in Zephyr. I toss my hoodie and T-shirt in the clothes dryer and walk out front again.

"That's your color," Grace says as I slide back into the booth. She tells me when she washed the jersey, she was missing me. She got curious and researched Diego Forlán. Read all about him. Watched his highlights on YouTube. "Looks like Samson with those golden locks. He backed it up. That fool could bend it like Beckham."

"Yeah he could."

"And the way he educates people about his sister's paralysis. His driving-safety message. Charities. All that."

"For sure," I say.

"Diego's dad and grandpa were Uruguayan soccer gods. Forlán had a path to glory paved for him before he was even born. You know who I really like?"

"Please don't say Lionel Messi."

"Luis Suárez. He plays angry. Like a rabid pit bull with his butt on fire."

"You did your research," I say.

"You were gone a long time," she says.

"He's a great scorer. But you like him more than Forlán? Suárez bites people."

"Only three times," she says, laughing. "And he only head-butted one youth soccer ref that we know of." She leans in. "There's no excuse for biting your opponent. But there might be reasons. You ever read that article about where he grew up?"

I shake my head.

Grace tells the story as well as she remembers it. Suárez grew up poor in a tough neighborhood. He wanted out. Soccer was the ticket. But to get noticed, you had to win. And you had to be the best. Little Luis learned that being nice wasn't a part of that equation. Desperation was. Taking a dive was. Kicking ankles. Grabbing. Clawing. It wasn't soccer, it was survival.

That style worked. Luis got out of the neighborhood. Made it to Liverpool in the Premier League. But the neighborhood didn't leave Luis. He's played his whole career like a dog biting his way out of an alley fight.

I tell Grace my abuelo Hector talked about that Uruguayan grit. He said it's the *Garra Charrúa* within Uruguayan players that gives them the edge they need to compete against more talented teams from much bigger countries. He told me the story of the Charrúa, Indigenous people who lived on the land that's now Uruguay, how they put up a courageous fight against the worst odds when the Europeans showed up with horses and guns and cannons.

Sure, it's messed up that they use the Charrúa's tenacity to describe how descendants of those Europeans play *a game*. But the way Uruguayans see their team, and the way the players see themselves—as underdogs who will never give up in a fight, no matter the odds—that is one hundred percent real.

"You got some of that grit in you," Grace says.

"Yeah," I say. "Maybe."

"No maybe," she says. "You and me, we are more Suárez than Forlán. We had to be. Because of the lives we were born into."

I think about all the times Suárez has been suspended. And the chances he's gotten to come back and to prove he can be both a world-class soccer player and a decent human being.

Grace sets her coffee cup on the table. "I hurt a lot of people on my way to surviving."

"He's in his thirties, Grace."

"I'm seventy! I still have years of mistakes left in me. I just hope there are people left to forgive me when I make my next mistake, people who think I'm worth another shot. Plus, it's been years since Suárez bit anyone, years since he's been suspended. I've been good for a few years too. People grow up, Antonio. They finally begin to realize they've already survived. And they look outside themselves and see that there are people in their lives who love them and care deeply about them and just need them to be there. To be *here*."

"I'm sorry I disappointed you," I say. "Sorry I never reached out to you from Zephyr. I could have called. I could have explained. I should have. It's just..."

She takes a sip. And she waits.

I want to tell her she was the only one who treated me like I was worth something. And I was too embarrassed, too ashamed, to tell her she was wrong.

"I don't know why you robbed," she says. "There's no excuse. But I'm sure there were reasons."

The way this lady looks at me. Her eyes. Her smile.

"But I swear on my life, Antonio Sullivan, if you ever do anything like that again, I will kill you. Do you hear me?"

"What about forgiveness?" I tease her. "What about second chances?"

"I won't kill you, Antonio. And hey, when the sale finally goes through, those potheads are going to need someone to train them on doughnuts. We'll write a managerial position into the sales contract for you. You'll make money for college. *College.* Imagine that, Antonio. You could be the doctor or lawyer or engineer grandson I never had. No pressure, of course."

I tell Grace maybe I'll take her up on that offer. Then I tell her about my meeting at Puget. I ask her if she can come.

"Yes!" she says. "Of course. When?"

"Seven AM. Tomorrow morning."

"What are you doing here, then? You go home and get to bed, young man!"

"Okay," I say, scooting out of the booth. "I'm going."

She grabs me by the arm. "You and me, Antonio?"

"Yeah, Grace?"

"We're good."

I hadn't realized how bad I needed to hear that. All I can do is nod to keep from crying.

"Now go!"

I grab my clothes out of the dryer. I take off my jersey. Put my hoodie on and pull my jersey over it.

The bell tinkles as Westernco's doors close behind me.

I inhale deep.

I exhale slow and pat the shield over my heart. And I take my next steps into the cold, wet night, toward Pac Highway and another long walk across town.

SUNDAY `10:36 PM`

I'm standing at my dad's front door, panting after the uphill walk, my jersey soaked from rain and sweat.

The rumble of an engine interrupts the quiet night.

I turn to see a big dark truck creeping up 6th Street. Creeping my way. *It's maroon.* It flashes its high beams and just sits there. *It's Murdock. Tracking me down.* My heart pounds in my chest and in my throat. The truck finally passes the house and turns into the next driveway. A delivery guy pops out with a pizza.

My relief lasts only a second because I have no idea how I'll get out of here with what I need. It's too big a risk. And what if I get back to the marina and I'm wrong about the money being under the burn mark?

I take in the deepest breath I can.

I exhale slow and think this through. *I can't get into trouble. I can't get sent away. I've already survived. My crazy childhood. Juvie. Zephyr Woods. Now I'm out. I'm free. There are people who love me. They need me here. And they need me alive.*

I turn to leave.

But the door flies open. "Antonio!"

Before I can run, my dad springs my way and grabs me by the arm. A current of electricity shoots from his clenched fingers into my arms, all over my body.

"You're safe!" he says, loud enough for the neighborhood to hear. I try to pull away, to run, to go straight back home and put an end to this night and this stupid plan. But my dad yanks me into his chest and hugs me tight. I'm suffocating in his arms, his beer breath and sweat. That electric current surges into me again.

I wrench myself out of the hug, but he manages to keep an arm wrapped tight around my shoulders.

"Thank you, Jesus." He squeezes harder. "I was tracking you. You were all over town. Out of town. To the airport. Zigging and zagging. I was terrified they had you."

"Who had me?"

"Lance and Rock! Do you know what that guy does for a living?"

"Rock?"

"He makes people do things they don't want to. If they refuse, he hurts them. Boy, do I know it."

"Dad, you're smothering me. Could you just—"

He walks me back toward the front door. "They've got that kid Vaughn. Who knows what they'll do to him to get the money. Even after they have it, they might—Wait, how are you here and your phone is—"

"I lost it. That's why I came early. I was afraid you'd go look-ing for me."

"I was about to. But I got so worried about you, so anxious, that I...drank."

"Where's Nancy?"

"Her sister's place in Bellevue."

That's a relief. If she were here, this whole thing would be a lot harder.

"Nancy doesn't know," he says. "She can't know."

"Know what?"

"That I am"—he flashes air quotes—"inebriated." He closes the front door and starts walking me toward the garage. "I feel compelled to explain."

"You really don't—"

"Let me finish!" he says. "No one lets me finish."

"Go ahead. Please."

"Are you absolutely certain it is okay for me to speak?"

I nod.

"I am grateful for the opportunity." He pokes the code into a keypad on the wall outside the garage. As the door rises, we're slowly bathed in light.

He puts a finger to his temple. "Where was I?"

"Inebriated."

"Right! I live a sober life, Antonio. The steps. The higher power. Who knew I'd end up falling for Jesus? And fall in love with my sponsor, Nancy. I have AA to thank for everything I've got."

"Sounds good."

"But sometimes I get real anxious, and I can't stop the hamster wheel from spinning, you know?" He whistles and points a wiggling finger at his head. "So if Nancy's not here, and I don't have to work the next morning, I pop a beer or two to recalibrate."

"That's interesting."

"Isn't it? Drinking used to be about chaos and dysfunction. Now it's about mindfulness."

"You've come a long way."

"AA saved my life. But the all-or-nothing part—"

"The not-drinking part?"

"Uh-huh."

"That's a big part, Dad."

"Doesn't work for me. Now," he says, guiding me inside the garage, "I invite you to join me for a beer in the grotto, where we can toast to being alive."

I wanna run. I wanna sprint straight home. But I can't shake the image of my mom's face as she glared at me from the window. Disgust. Disappointment. If she were here right now she'd be throwing my dad that exact same look. There is no going back until I can change the way she sees me.

"A toast sounds good," I say. "I could really use a drink."

He rolls a tool cabinet on wheels away from the wall. Then he opens a small door, revealing a refrigerator that's just big enough to hold a mini keg and a couple frosty beer mugs.

I turn to my right to check out those garden tools hanging on the wall. The shovels and rakes.

I step around the hood of the Miata. Steal a peek in through the open driver's-side window. The keys are still in the ignition.

"Nuts?" He offers me a tiny bag of almonds. I step back around the front of the car and pocket the nuts. He hands me the massive, freezing-cold mug. I tilt it back. The beer pours into my mouth. I don't swallow. I let it wash back into the mug. "Ahh...tasty."

"Miller Lite."

"Nice."

I just have to wait for my chance. It's about a ten-minute drive to the pier. I'm guessing I need an hour to get the job done—I want two hours just to be sure. Gary and Vaughn—and probably Lance—will be getting there at one thirty. I should be outta there by one o'clock so there's no possible way I run into them and so I have plenty of time to make it to Westernco by one thirty to meet up with Claudio.

I ask my dad for the time.

"It is officially," he says, "quarter past time to drain my main vein."

"Wow, Dad."

"If you'd be so kind as to excuse me." He takes a step toward the house door, then stops. "Don't go anywhere," he says.

"I won't."

"You're a good boy, Antonio."

When the door closes behind him, I set the mug down fast. I grab boxes and pile them in front of the door to slow him down when he comes back.

I dash over to check the Miata's trunk. It's locked. I reach in the open window and pull out the keys. I unlock the trunk and start loading. I toss in the shovel and rake. Their handles hang out the back. Lawn bags. An extension cord I can use as rope. It's long. Maybe fifty feet. I throw it in there and leave the lid up.

I skip around to the driver's-side door, slip a finger in the latch, pop it open, and drop myself into the front seat. I reach up to the visor and hit the button on the garage-door opener.

Left foot on the clutch. Turn the key. Shift left and up.

I glance at the rearview and—*dammit!*—the door is going back down. The boxes didn't stop him. He's standing in the doorway, his finger on the button, shaking his head, disappointed, exhausted.

I drop my forehead onto the steering wheel.

He walks over to the driver's side. Bends over. "Where you going, bud?"

I shrug my shoulders.

"You're going nowhere in Nancy's car. Not with shovels. Not to dig up that money. *Lance* is going to get that money. And if Lance has the money, that means you are safe. I messed up your life before. I'm not letting you mess it up tonight. *Out.*"

I can't move.

He reaches through the open window and takes the keys out of the ignition. Slips them in his pocket. "So your friends told you they buried the money, huh? Same friends that got you sent to prison. You think maybe it's time for new friends?"

"What did they do with the money, then?"

"They sank it in a crab pot off Vashon Island."

I just nod. I don't know what game Vaughn's playing. But Gary isn't lying. The money's buried at the pier.

"That Vaughn hates you and Gary. He told Lance everything."

He leans inside the car window with both hands, forgetting he's still holding his beer. He spills all over me. My face, my jeans, my jersey. There's beer all over the seat and the floor of the car.

"Aw hell. Nancy will kill me! We gotta clean it up. We gotta get that smell out." The mug thuds when he sets it on the convertible top. He turns away to grab a rag.

I pop out of the car, reach up for the mug. I grip the handle tight in my fist. I take a step closer to him, pulling my arm back as far as I can.

He rotates around so he's facing me, his terrified eyes catching mine.

And in the moment before...time freezes.

I come home from school. He's drunk. Crying. He says he went to see Mom. He says she wouldn't let him in the house. He says Tammy called the cops on him. He says it like it's my fault. He grabs me. He throws me against the wall. I try to lock eyes with him. I shout, "No!" Doesn't stop his hand from pushing my neck into the wall, his fingers, his nails, digging in. His other hand, a flying fist, knuckles crunching my cheek. He holds me there. Still by the neck. He looks into my eyes. I want to fight back. I want to. I'm too small. Too afraid. Too tired.

I want this to end. Barely any air, I manage to get out the words. "Kill me."

He releases my neck, crying, "No, Antonio. No."
My dad sobs as he apologizes over and over. Just like all the times before.

"No, Antonio!" he shouts as he catches sight of my shoulder rotating, my arm swinging, my hand shooting forward, the mug blasting his face with a thud.

He's on the ground, moaning, writhing.

I slip my hand in his pocket and pull out the keys. I step toward the car.

A jolt of electricity shoots up my leg. His hands are gripped around my calf.

I kick free. Kick him in the ribs. Drop back into the seat. Slam the door. Hit the garage-door opener. Slip the key in the ignition.

He's up on his knees now.

I press the clutch.

"Don't go, Antonio! You're safe here!" he shouts, spitting blood.

Turn the key.

"Don't go!"

Shift left and up.

He reaches out, lunges, and grabs the door.

Release the clutch!

I hit the gas hard. Tires squeal. I watch him fall. Then I duck as the garage door skims the convertible top and I'm shot out onto the street.

I pound the clutch. Then the brake. Shift into first. I flip the headlights on and I'm staring right at her. Nancy in the driver's seat of a blue Ford Focus. Big blond hair. Mouth wide open in shock, watching me take off in her Miata. Her eyes shift to the open garage. My dad is standing, arms waving, face bloody, eyes on fire.

I floor it out of there. Down 6th. Left on 207th. Right on Marine View Drive.

Breathe, Antonio.

I try to. But an image in the windshield takes my breath away. His face. Staring at me. A reflection. A ghost. This version of my dad with his soft eyes full of love. The man who played heroes and villains with me, the dad who saved those comics for me, who wrote that inscription to me, the dad who took care of my mom.

His mouth opens. His lips move. But it's my mind feeding him the lines.

> *I hit your mom, Antonio. I hurt her. I know you saw me do it. I hit you. Neglected you. I forced you to drink with me. Forced you to deliver to Lance for me. I made you feel like a bad person. Made you feel worthless. Made you feel small. Said horrible things about your mom. Said horrible things about your friends. Said horrible things about you. Made you feel like I was the best you deserved. Made you live your life in fear and desperation. You had a spark when you were young. You had joy in you. I smothered that. I need you to know I'm sorry.*
>
> *I need forgiveness, Antonio. Forgive me. Forgive me.*

I breathe deep. And I say the words strong, right into the windshield.

"Life got to be too much. You tried. You failed miserably. I understand failing miserably. I'm forgiving you. I'm letting go. Anger. Hatred. Fear. All that. Letting go of it. I forgive you, Dad. I forgive you. I forgive you.

"But this is it. The end of you needing to ask for it. The end of me needing to grant it. Because this is goodbye. Forever. Go live your life. I'll go live mine. Goodbye, Dad. Goodbye. Goodbye. Goodbye." I say it over and over until his face fades away.

SUNDAY 11:14 PM

I dart into a parking spot in front of the big condo building on Cliff Avenue, just across the street from the closed entrance to the marina parking lot. I slip on my backpack and run to the trunk to grab the shovel, extension cord, and bags. I'm exposed by flood-lights as I make my way around the parking-gate arm, lugging everything across the lot, fast as I can, rain pelting my face.

At the second light post from the pier, I toss the stuff over the edge and climb the railing. I hop down. A *slup* sound as I land in the mud.

I wrap my way around the pilings, scrambling underneath in the darkness and up the back beach. I pull out my phone—Claudio's phone—swiping and thumbing the flashlight. I point it up to the underside of the pier planks, then walk, water dripping onto my face. I locate the black char mark, and my heart gets pumping hard and fast.

I check the time. I have to be out of here in two hours. I have to dig, pull out the bags, haul them back to the car, load them up, and go. If the bags are buried in this spot, I'm a genius. If they're not...

I slip off my backpack and toss it to the side. I center myself under the mark. I pocket the phone. It's dark. But there's enough light from the pier lampposts bleeding through the planks.

I grab the shovel and grip the handle in two fists at my chest. Raise it up, up, up, till my fists are above my head. Then slam it into the earth. I push the handle down like a lever, almost to the ground, pulling up pounds of mud, sand, and rock. Then I lift and dump it to the side.

I do that fifty times, and it looks like I've barely done anything at all.

I check the time. I close my eyes.

The sound of the tide rolling in. I inhale and raise the shovel high.

The sound of the tide pulling out. I pound the shovel down.

I lever, lift, and dump.

Tide in, raise up.

Tide out, pound down.

Lever, lift, dump.

Tide in, raise.

Tide out, pound.

It goes on like that until I'm not thinking about the tide or the shovel or the hole or my tired, soaking feet or blistering fingers. I'm thinking about my mom, imagining her face, sending her the message that I'm on my way home. And this craziness is gonna be over soon. And I'm paying off her medical bills. And I'm paying for Claudio's addition to the house, or maybe even a whole new house. And I'm starting a college fund for Olivia. And I'm gonna keep bringing money in. Because I'll be the manager at Westernco Donut. And I'm gonna pay rent and utilities and for my share of the food.

And I'm gonna pay for someone to listen to me like Mrs. Williams did at Zephyr. And I'll tell that person the darkest parts of my story. And when they ask how it makes me feel, I'm straight up gonna tell them the truth so I may learn from my history so that I will not be doomed to repeat it. And when I feel overwhelmed and I can't think straight, that person will sit with me. Just sit with me. And be silent with me. And breathe with me. So I will not lash out or run away from my problems. I will calmly think and consider and take appropriate action.

I'm promising my mom that I will never break another house rule. I will never make an exit through a window. And I'll admit to my mom she was right about me seeing Maya. And there will be no more Maya drama. And Gary Jr. will never again be allowed to drag me or my family into his chaos.

And I'm never again dragging Claudio into my drama. Because there will be no drama. Because I'm never breaking another term. And I'm never going to hope things can go back to the way they were when I was little.

I'm going to grieve that life.

And get past the trauma that came after.

And embrace this beautiful new life full of family and opportunity.

I'm sending my mom mental messages of every single thing I'm thinking. Everything except...

WHOOOSH! White noise of the crashing tide floods my mind. *Lance!* I picture him coming after me for the money. He's furious. He's got a knife. He's got a gun. He's pointing. Cocking it.

Stop, Antonio! I drop the shovel and swat the side of my head to stop the thought. Cuz I can't send my mom that message. But what if—what if he—what if he—

Stop!

And listen.

The sound of the tide rolling in. I raise the shovel high.

The sound of the tide pulling out. I pound the shovel down.

Tide in, raise up.

Tide out, pound down.

Lever, lift, dump.

Tide in, raise.

Tide out, pound.

Lever, lift, dump.

FRIDAY

SATURDAY

SUNDAY

MONDAY

I finally hit something.

Tide in, raise up.

Tide out, pound down.

Lever, lift, dump.

Tide in, raise up—Wait! What? I hit something?

I hit something!

I toss the shovel to the side. Fall to my knees. Heart pounding, belly in the mud, I thrust my hand down. Reach for it. *Waaaay* down into the deep hole. Tips of my fingers in muddy water, I'm feeling it. *Nylon!* I grab for a handle. Yup, it's a dry bag! And there's gotta be a second one just below it.

I love you, Gary, for burying this money in the most obvious possible place. But obvious to only one person in the entire world. Me!

I check the time.

One hour till they show up. I got half an hour to dig around the bags enough to pull them out. Twenty minutes to haul them to the car and make it on time to meet Claudio at Westernco.

I lift the shovel high.

When I Got a Life

So then, dawn arrived in the Westernco back room.
My alarm rang, and I rose from the futon for my training with Tommy.

I got my hands messy in grease, flour, sugar,
yeast, food coloring, natural—and unspeakably unnatural—flavors.

In the mornings that followed, I was rolling, cutting,
mixing, baking, frying, boiling, icing,
gaining confidence every day
while waiting to get off suspension
and waiting to hear from Gary and Vaughn.

But I only heard from my dad.
He didn't ask me where I was staying.
Didn't ask me to come home.
Just told me Gary and Vaughn got arrested.
Lance too, and he was afraid he might be next.

Do you know how they got the keys?

I don't, I say.

Grace and Tommy fed me well.
There was a shower. A washer and dryer.
Clean sheets. A warm comforter. A fluffy pillow.

It wasn't the life I'd imagined.
But for once, I was living a life.

I scrape mud and rock, chipping it away from around the sides of the bag. Widening the hole. Down on my knees, on my stomach, pulling rocks out with my bare hands. I tug and tug with every ounce of strength I have left until I'm shining light on the two bags sitting in the mud. They're zipped up and rolled tight at the top, just like they're supposed to be to keep water from seeping in. Between them and the plastic trash bags Gary and Vaughn stuffed the money in, maybe the bills will still be dry after all this time under mud and tides.

I wrap an end of the extension cord around the middle of one bag so when I haul it to the second lamp pole, I can use it to hoist the bag up off the beach and over the pier railing.

Before I go, I pull out Claudio's phone to check the time. There's a string of messages from my mom to me that Claudio has forwarded from my phone to his.

Hey Antonio. Praying you're all right.
Forwarding messages to you from your mom:

(FWD)
¡Te quiero, Antonio! Come home.
¡Te necesito aquí¡ I need you here with
me. There is nothing else. Just you and
your sister in my arms.

(FWD)
YOU AND OLIVIA ARE EVERYTHING TO
ME! YOU ARE ALL I NEED. I DON'T CARE
YOU SNUCK OUT. I DON'T CARE YOU
SAW YOUR DAD. I DON'T CARE YOU SAW
MAYA. NO IMPORTA! ALL THAT MATTERS IS
US TOGETHER. SOLO ESO!

(FWD)
Everything else we can manage. We can talk
through. We belong together. I swear I can be
the mom you need. I promise. I just need a
chance. Just come home!
This is your home. Come home!

(FWD)
I LOVE YOU ANTONIO!

I think it right back to her. But I can't text her. Not yet.

I check the time. *One twenty-five.* My heart stops. I was supposed to be gone by now. Gone before Gary. Before Vaughn and

Lance. I was supposed to be at Westernco to see Claudio. The blood rushes from my face. My breath races away and I can't—I can't—I can't—catch—

Stop.

Close your eyes.

Inhale deep, Antonio.

Nope! I got no time for breathing. I have to haul these massive bags, one at a time, up the beach, over the rail, across the parking lot, across the street, and into the Miata. If Gary and Lance and Vaughn are on time, they'll catch me for sure.

I can't risk it.

I look at the bags and think.

They're black.

The water at night is black.

I reach down for the bag I'd just tied up. I bend my knees, lift, and haul it out from underneath the pier and down to the waterline. I run back underneath and grab the shovel.

I tie the middle of the cord around the base of the shovel. Then I grip the shovel handle in my two fists at my chest. I lift it to the sky. And I pound it down as far as it'll go. I jump on the metal base of the shovel. I hop up and down, pushing it deeper into mud and rock. I scan the beach for the biggest rocks I can find. I pile six or seven of them on top, where the metal base of the shovel meets wood handle.

I run back under the pier. Bend knees. Lift bag. Scoot my ass back to the edge of the water. Tie the second bag with the other end of the extension cord. These bags are made to float. I launch the first bag into the water. Then the other.

They float! And they're barely visible. And probably, maybe, hopefully, not visible at all if you don't already know they're there.

I turn away from the water to make my escape, but I immediately hear his voice.

"Tonio! Vaughn! Tonio!" Gary is standing at that second lamppost, scanning the pier and beach with a flashlight.

"Gary!" I rush up the beach right at him. "Stay there! Don't come down! I'll come up there!"

"What the hell, Tonio?"

I wave my arms, desperately trying to prevent Gary from spotting the floating dry bags. And to keep him from heading under the pier and discovering the massive empty hole.

I make it to the lamppost and climb the rail.

Gary leans over and shouts, "We were supposed to meet at the gate!"

"Quiet down," I say, climbing up to the top, then flying over the rail.

Immediately, I'm bent over, hands on knees, panting, exhausted from shoveling, running, climbing. "Sorry I made you wait," I say. "I was down—I thought I would—like old times—Forget it. I'll explain later. We gotta get outta here before Lance and Vaughn show up in that boat."

"Lance? A boat? You said there was no boat!"

I stand upright. "I lied. I'm telling the truth now. I think there's a boat. We gotta go!"

"Tonio," he says, "the part of me that knows you are a loving, loyal friend is telling me, *Trust your bud.* But the smart part of me says you are trying to screw me over."

We hear the roar of an engine, a boat approaching beyond the faraway end of the pier.

"Lance is in that boat! Come on!" I sprint toward the gate.

Gary follows close, shouting, "We can't leave Vaughn! He wouldn't do that to us!"

The roar stops as the engine is cut.

We keep on running and are just yards from getting through the parking gate when we hear the words "*STOP OR I'LL SHOOT!*"

We stop and thrust trembling hands in the air.

"Turn this way real slow!" The voice coming from the pier isn't Lance's or Vaughn's. It's gotta be Rock's.

We do as we're told. Arms kept high. Slowly rotating.

And I'm thinking I'm the only one who knows where the money is. And the money is the only thing Lance cares about. If I tell him where it is, then I'm off the hook. Lance is out of my life forever. Vaughn is out of my life forever. And Gary Jr. too.

Tell Lance where the dry bags are.

Go drop the car off in Normandy Park.

Walk home.

Apologize to mom. Apologize to Claudio. Hug Olivia.

Make my meeting on time.

Make amends to Maya and my mom by living my best life.

We turn to face Rock. He's standing in the middle of the pier, half his face in shadow, the other half lit up by lamplight. "Walk this way," he says. "Slow and easy."

When you get close enough that you don't have to shout, calmly tell Rock you need to talk to Lance. Then point at the bags floating in the water and say, "The money is right there." Then you can go home. And everything will be okay.

We're close enough that we can see Rock's wire-rimmed glasses and his old-school Sounders beanie and green windbreaker. He's short. He's got chubby red cheeks and a paunch. He's probably my dad's age. Rock would never be cast as a movie thug.

"Where you running away to?" Rock says.

We don't answer.

"I'm gonna need you to follow instructions from here on out. Understood?"

"Yes," I say, still walking slowly, my voice shaking. "Could I please talk to—"

"Down the ladder. Now!" It's Lance's voice.

Gary keeps walking. I freeze and shout, "Wait!" I point toward the northern tip of Vashon Island and the imaginary crab pot. "The money's not—"

"The money's not *what*?" Lance says, poking his head up from the ladder.

Oh my God. My heart. My racing breath. That fake-tan face. That twisted, smarmy smirk. Like he thinks he's the smartest person in the world.

"The money's not what? Talk to me, *Antonio*."

That sneering tone when he says my name. Same way he's always said it. Like I'm less than nobody. Just the loser son of his loser employee.

I close my eyes.

I inhale deep.

I exhale slow and shake my head. *Nope. Uh-uh. That's not his money. It came from . . .* The image pops into my mind. That zombie face at Lance's door. That ghost I can't outrun, can't breathe away. That *person.*

Lost.

His eyes. His face. A thousand faces. Lost faces.

Their money.

Antonio, if you tell him where the money is, that's you choosing fear.

Choosing Lance.

Choosing your dad.

Again.

A scared kid delivering bad men their money.

Again.

People you know need that money. Your mamá. Claudio. Olivia.

Lance is standing up on the pier now, facing me. "The money's not *what, Antonio?*" He sneers my name again.

"Yours," I say. "The money is not yours."

Lance cracks up laughing. "So brave, Antonio! So courageous! Now, down you go." His face disappears as he descends into the boat.

Rock keeps the gun trained on us as we pass him. I lower my hands slowly to grasp the top of the ladder. I swing one leg over. Then the other.

I hear a chirp of a whistle above me. I lift my chin and I'm face-to-face with Gary Jr. He smiles at me, juts his chin, and winks. He's telling me we're good. And we're on the same page again. And everything is going to work out.

That's Gary Jr.

I jut my chin back at him, wink, and climb into the boat.

"Hi, Antonio." It's Vaughn. The interior boat lights are bright enough that I can make out his pained smile, those annoying dimples, that most punchable face. He's taller. More filled out. His new, fit body is hugged by an equally new North Face jacket. A crisp haircut. He reaches out to guide me over the chrome railing, and his grip—dude has been working out. He gestures to the white-leather, upholstered bench seating at the rear of this gorgeous twenty-foot Boston Whaler.

As I take my seat, he makes eye contact, like he's trying to send a message.

But I can't make it out. And if I could, I wouldn't trust it anyway.

Vaughn shakes his head and steps up on the bench, reaching up to the pier ladder to help Gary down.

Gary takes a seat next to me, nudging my arm, his expression asking, *What the hell is going on?*

Lance sits at the bow, legs crossed, facing us. He's got a little pistol strapped to his hip.

He smiles at me across the boat, his tiny lips sneering.

I want to smack that smug face.

Rock climbs in last. He stands before us, reaches into his pocket, and pulls out a bunch of long zip ties. He hands them to Vaughn.

Vaughn approaches us, smiling, dimples popping. "What do you think of the Whaler, guys? Surprised?"

"Extremely," Gary says.

"Because you two never believed in me." He shakes a zip tie at Gary. "Wrists out."

Gary Jr. does as he's told. As Vaughn leans in and wraps the tie around his wrists, Gary whispers, "I know you're doing this against your will."

Vaughn grimaces at Gary as he threads the end of the zip tie through the loop. Holding the end of the tie, he stands tall. Lifts a foot and rests it on the bench. "Here we go!" Vaughn *yanks* the tie back with two hands, like he's starting an old lawn mower.

"Jesus *effing* Christ! What the hell, Vaughn?"

Vaughn stares at him, stone-cold. "I am *not* on your side."

Rock snickers at that.

Vaughn kneels and ties one around Gary's ankles. He stands, saying, "I been waiting a long time for this." He pulls an open-palmed hand way back.

"No!" Gary shouts as Vaughn's arm shoots forward, slapping him in the face so hard, his head flies and knocks into mine, his body slamming into my shoulder.

Gary turns to his old buddy, tears streaming down his face. He rubs his cheek with zip-tied fists. "Are you serious, Vaughn?"

"Dead serious! You were never going to cut me in! When Lance called and promised me my share, I was like, *Lemme get this straight. You're asking me to trick idiot Gary and idiot Antonio into leading you to that crab pot where all the money is? Hell yes! Where do I sign up?*"

"Crab pot?" Gary says. "Really?"

"Screw you both! You were jerks to me! You called me *idiot Vaughn* behind my back. Who's the idiot now?" He slaps Gary again harder.

"Holy freaking freak, Vaughn!"

"Answer me, Gary!"

"I'm the idiot now! Okay?" Gary jerks his chin my way. "It was him who started that whole *idiot Vaughn* thing, FYI."

Vaughn turns to me. "Wrists." He wraps them. Threads the end through. A foot up on the bench.

I close my eyes.

I inhale dee—

Holy hell! It's like he's trying to pull my arms out of their sockets. He steps back so he's got enough space for a full swing, and…

My neck snaps back. Ears ringing. The world is a blur.

"Idiot Antonio!" he shouts at the top of his lungs.

I move my jaw from side to side, trying to line it up with the rest of my head. I press palms against my ears to stop the ringing.

Vaughn zip-ties my ankles, then jumps onto the ladder. He unspools the rope from the metal cleat at the top of the pier. Then he steps down onto the bench between me and Gary and hops to the cockpit in the center of the boat. He takes the wheel, fires up the engine, and pulls us away from the pier.

Gary and me share a glance as we watch the distance between land and us grow, not knowing when, or if, we'll ever step foot on that pier again.

"Hey, idiot Gary!" Vaughn shouts over the engine noise. "I'm taking us to the north end of the island. If you do not direct us to that crab pot, Rock will direct you to Davy Jones's locker."

"Love the enthusiasm!" Rock shouts. "But *Davy Jones's locker*? That's too much."

"Is it the killing that's wrong?" Vaughn says. "Or the phrase?"

"The killing part is on point. Just nix the *Davy Jones*. That's lame pirate cheese."

"Good note," Vaughn says, glaring at us. "I'll just be like, *Rock will shoot you and throw you overboard.*"

"Getting warmer, kid. But keep in mind I only fire my gun as a last resort."

"That's a relief," Gary says.

Rock calmly explains that if things were to go south, he would zip-tie our ankle zip ties to our wrist zip ties so we're folded up good. Then he'd toss us over the side of the boat. "Quieter than firing rounds," he says. "No cleanup. And I don't have to watch death happen."

"Got it," Vaughn says. "If ever I must kill, I will kill in a way that is not loud or messy and I don't have to watch the idiot's life drain from his—"

"Jesus Christ!" Lance says. "No one is getting killed! All right?" He turns to me and Gary. "Just get us to that crab pot. We'll pull it up, take the money out, and drop you off at the ferry. As long as you two stay quiet, Rock will stay out of your lives forever."

Vaughn kicks the Whaler into high gear. He's got the boat aimed at Dolphin Point, miles ahead. We skim the waves, bouncing, cold salt water spraying our faces.

My knees start shaking, my stomach turning. Not from motion sickness but from worry about what happens when Lance finds out the money is not in that crab pot.

Vaughn is leading us to something. He has to be. He has a plan. *Trust Vaughn.*

I can't trust Vaughn.

You have to trust him.

His plan can't be good.

Trust him.

Because Vaughn is an idiot. Who screwed up the robbery. Who screwed me over in court. Who ruined my life.

I close my eyes.

And I consider the possibility that this might be the night I die, sinking into the murky, cold silence of Puget Sound.

I think about my mom's house. Just her and Claudio and Olivia. I think about my mom never understanding what happened to me the weekend I came home from Zephyr Woods. Never understanding what I tried to do, how I tried to make amends to her.

I think about Olivia growing up without her brother. Always wondering about me. About the loser, the thief, who went to prison, was released, then immediately got himself messed up in another crime. And was murdered. She could grow up thinking her brother was a criminal. Or a victim. She might be sad about what happened to me. Or feel sorry for me. Or dismiss my existence because in the story of her life, I just didn't matter.

My eyes pop open. There are tiny lights twinkling from inside waterfront homes on Maury Island to the southwest and Vashon to the north. I keep my eyes on those lights as I imagine surviving this night.

I'll miss my meeting. I'll get sent back to Zephyr Woods. The worst part is, it will be that much harder to fix things with my mom. Maybe I'll even lose my shot at living with her when I get out again.

I imagine Olivia the moment she's old enough to be told that her brother lives in prison.

I see Maya's face when she finds out I'm back there. Grace's too. And Mrs. Williams's and Ms. Duncan's. All so disappointed. I picture Mrs. Neville shaking her head as she watches me get hauled inside those doors in handcuffs again.

I would take all that disappointment. Because it would mean I made it through this night alive. With a chance to become something better.

Vaughn takes the engine down a notch. "Hey, idiot Gary! Should I be looking for the crab pot south of Dolphin Point or north of Dolphin Point?"

Gary freezes at the question, then turns to me, wide-eyed. I elbow him in the ribs. He turns back to Vaughn and says, "Why would there be a crab pot on the north side?"

"I was groggy the night we sank the money. I don't know where it is," Vaughn says. "You do."

"Yeah," Gary says, "you were messed up, but we didn't go anywhere near—"

I elbow Gary harder.

"Okay. Right. The currents are too strong on the north. Only commercial crabbers out there, so..."

"So we go south of the ferry dock?"

"Yes, Vaughn. South of the ferry dock."

Vaughn turns the wheel and aims the Boston Whaler due south of the Vashon ferry dock. He gives it gas, and in seconds we're flying again across relatively calm waters. We're going to get there soon. Too soon.

Lance's eyes are trained in the same direction as the boat—out where he thinks his money is waiting for him. For a second, Rock takes his eyes off us and looks out there too.

Gary leans into my shoulder and whispers, "What's Vaughn doing?"

I purse my lips and shake my aching head to shut him up.

I scan the boat for a flare gun to alert another boat. Even if there was something, it wouldn't matter, because Rock is watching us again.

I try to twist my wrists, to see if I can free them, but the zip ties dig in and cut my skin. My head aches and my ears ring from Vaughn's slap.

Me and Gary Jr. got no options. There is no way. We're zip-tied kids against men with guns—and Vaughn and this ridiculous game he's playing.

Rock points the gun at my jersey. Gives me a thumbs-up. "Forlán!" he says, leaning forward and shouting to be heard. "I used to follow him at Atlético de Madrid. He had a cannon right foot and a cannon left. Not too many guys like that."

I nod. Fake smile.

"Long gone now," he says. "You know who I really like?"

"Luis Suárez?"

"*Suárez?* Ha! He's an over-the-hill, undisciplined madman!" Rock gets an evil grin on his face and says, "Lionel Messi is where it's at! He's a damn god."

I shake my head with a scowl. It's not just that Argentina is our biggest rival, it's that Messi is too obvious. He's the most talented player in the world. From a country twelve times the size of Uruguay. There was a path to greatness and World Cup championships laid out for tiny Lionel the second a scout watched him slalom the ball from one end of a youth soccer pitch to the other.

Rock sees the look on my face and chants, *"Messi! Messi!"* pointing that gun right at me. *"Messi! Messi!"*

I close my eyes and breathe through the taunting and laughing. *"Messi! Messi!"*

My jaw tightens, my abs tighten, my muscles clench.

Breathe, Antonio.

I do not care if the odds are against us.

Breathe, Antonio.

I shake off Mrs. Williams's voice in my head as Lance flashes me that smarmy grin and Rock laughs and laughs.

Something in my gut rumbles. And it grows. And it takes me over. I chirp a whistle at Gary. I jut my chin at him again, just like he'd done to me.

Gary Jr. chirps a whistle back, winks at me, and juts his chin back one more time.

I don't know how we're gonna do it, but there is no way these assholes are gonna take us down. We will get past this night. We will survive. We will get off this boat. Because we have tenacity. We have instincts. We have grit forged in the fires of hunger, desperation, and teenage fuckuppery.

Me and Gary Jr...we are Luis Suárez.

"Idiot Gary!" Vaughn shouts, slowing the engine again to be

heard. "That buoy, I remember it was either black or orange, am I right?"

"Orange," Gary says, like it's the most obvious thing in the world. Day or night, in these dark waters, a black buoy would be near impossible to see. Gary flashes his eyes toward Vaughn and nods. He finally gets what Vaughn's doing. And he's going to play the game.

"It had reflectors," Vaughn says. "Am I right on that? A couple reflectors? Was it one or two?"

No reason to say *a couple* if there aren't more than one. I send Gary the mental message.

"Definitely two reflectors," he says. "No doubt about it."

Vaughn turns to Gary. "Hey, idiot, did that buoy have three red stripes?"

"That's right. It's coming back to you now," Gary says. "Orange buoy. Two reflectors. Three red stripes. You got it, Vaughn."

Gary turns to me and shrugs. He played the game. But what happens next? *Is there really a buoy? Is there really a crab pot? How can there be money in it?*

Vaughn cuts the engine way back so we're creeping toward land, near enough to make out the shapes of individual beach homes in the darkness.

There's a layer of fog on the sound. Lance grabs a big flashlight and goes to the bow of the boat. He shines it in the water. Scanning. Searching. We see rowboats and small motorboats tied to buoys. There are diving rafts for swimmers closer to the shore.

And there are buoys with nothing attached to them. Some of those lonely buoys have nylon ropes tied to them. The other ends of those ropes are attached to cages, crab pots anchoring the buoys to the floor of the sound, baited and waiting to trap an unsuspecting crab.

Vaughn points to the north. "The buoy was that way—right, Gary?"

"Right," Gary says.

"You check that way, then." He turns to me. "Idiot Antonio, you check south of the boat just in case. Orange buoy, two reflectors, two red stripes."

"Three stripes!" Gary says.

"Right," Vaughn says. "Three stripes."

Suddenly, Lance shines the light at a buoy and says, "There we go."

Orange. Three red stripes. One reflector shining back at us.

"Nope," Rock says.

Then the buoy rotates in the tide, revealing the second reflector.

And my heart.

Is.

Pounding in

my throat.

In

my head.

In

my fingers.

And I can't catch my racing breath. Cuz this is it. The moment we pull up a crab pot with zero dollars in it.

Gary freaks. He starts butt-jumping in his seat.

I knock my shoulder against his. His hops just get more frantic.

Rock lifts the gun barrel. Points it at Gary. "Cool it, kid."

We approach the buoy, just yards away now. There's a black bird standing on it. A cormorant, wings extended, frozen, like a gargoyle sentry guarding a castle. It's creepy.

But I take it as a good sign. Because me and Maya used to count them, and she'd record the number in her notepad. Almost always there're twenty or thirty cormorants when you're lucky enough to see them. I think about the day I can tell her me and Gary saw one solitary cormorant sitting on a buoy in the middle of the night.

Someday.

If we make it away from here alive.

Which we will.

Because we have fight in us.

We have tenacity.

We have grit.

Lance sets his flashlight down. He drops to his belly and slides his head and chest under the Whaler's railing. He leans out over the bow, face in the layer of fog, ready to catch the buoy.

The cormorant flies silently off into the mist.

"I got it!" Lance says, steadying the beach ball–size buoy with one hand, reaching into the water to grab the rope with the other.

Gary is hopping again, freaking out, as Vaughn steps over to the bow, then grabs the flashlight and shines it so Lance can see the rope in the water. Lance pulls, hand over fist, as fast as he can, raising the pot toward the surface.

He's still pulling when I hear the tiniest hum. It's a boat coming toward us from Dolphin Point. All I can see is its one beam of light slowly getting closer and closer.

My breath and heartbeat race.

Gary jumps faster, higher.

Vaughn leans over, staring at the rope lit up in the murky water. "The pot's almost up here," he says. I catch him sneak a peek at that approaching boat.

A thump each time Gary's butt lands on the bench. "It's the wrong buoy!" he shouts. "The wrong crab pot! There were three reflectors! Three, Vaughn!"

"Shut up, idiot!" Vaughn says.

"Boat," Rock says, motioning to Lance.

We're all looking in its direction now.

"We're just crabbers," Vaughn says. "Nothing suspicious. Just keep pulling that rope."

Gary gets up to his feet, wobbly, like he forgot his ankles were zip-tied.

"Sit down!" Rock commands, pushing Gary in the chest.

Gary's butt and back both thud as they hit the bench. "Stop pulling! It's the wrong pot! I was there! I should know!"

"Shut up!" Vaughn says.

"Stop pulling!" Gary shouts. "Stop pulling!"

Rock leans in, extending his gun hand and jabbing the barrel into Gary's thigh. "I will blast a hole in your leg if you don't shut—"

Gary hops to his feet again, daring Rock to shoot. "Stop this, Vaughn! Stop it!"

Rock pushes Gary in the chest to sit him down again. Gary thuds again.

My heart, my head, my breath. I can't let Rock push Gary. I will not let him shoot Gary.

Gary bounces back up. "Stop!" he shouts, his mouth foaming, as the wire-cage pot comes into view. "It's the wrong pot!"

I elbow Gary as hard as I can to shut him up.

As the pot comes into view, we make out a big metal box inside. It's wrapped in a clear plastic bag.

Vaughn heaves the pot onto the bow of the Whaler. Instead of reaching into the little cage door like you do to get crabs out, he pops some springs and pulls the whole top off by the handle. The sides of the pot collapse and crash onto the floor of the boat, exposing the metal box.

"That's not it!" Gary shouts. "It's the wrong one!"

"I am shooting you in *five*!" Rock shouts, shaking the gun at Gary.

"I was wrong!" Gary shouts. "I was wrong! It's all a lie!"

"I am shooting you in *four*," Rock shouts.

"Throw it back, Vaughn! Please! Please!"

"I am shooting you in *three*."

There's a huge Dungeness crab on top of the metal box. Vaughn reaches for it. "Agh!" He grabs it, pissed. "Damn thing pinched me!" He stands up tall, hops up onto the bench, and makes a big show of throwing the crab into the water as he watches that oncoming boat pick up speed.

Gary pops up again. "Stop! I was wrong!" Rock pushes. Gary thuds. "It's the wrong pot!" he shouts as Lance unwraps the plastic from the box.

"I swear to God, I am shooting you!" Rock shouts.

Lance pops latches on the box as the sound of the approaching boat crescendos.

I press my feet hard against the base of the bench.

"Wrong pot!" Gary shouts. "Wrong pot! Wrong pot!"

My heart, my head, my breath! I feel my feet push off the bottom of the boat.

"Shooting you in *one*!" Rock's finger tightens as he presses the gun into Gary's leg.

AGGGGGGHHHHH!

A bloody scream-shriek blasts out of me as I spring up and forward, flailing onto Rock, my zip-tied arms looping over his head, then wrapping tight around his face, sliding down his neck, and pulling the zip ties tight. And I sink my teeth into his shoulder.

Rock cries out in agony as he fires a deafening round into the bottom of the boat.

"What the hell, Rock?" Lance shouts.

The engine roar of the other boat. It's so close to us.

Rock flails, fighting to throw me off him with one hand and aim his gun with the other.

"Let go now, Tonio!"

I don't think. I just follow Gary's instruction. I jump and lift my arms back over Rock's head, releasing him just in time to see Gary—his back against the bench, legs cocked—kick the gun as it fires a deafening round and flies into the night sky.

We hear a *plop* and a sizzle of steam as the gun sinks down to Davy Jones's locker.

"Aw, hell no," Rock says, jumping forward and pulling the gun off Lance's holster.

Rock points this gun at Gary as Lance pops the last latch on the box.

In a split second, time freezes as the end of us flashes before my eyes.

Gary Jr. is shot dead by Rock.

I am shot dead by Rock.

There is nothing in that box.

Vaughn is shot dead by Rock.

The passengers in the oncoming boat, who are close enough to witness everything, are shot dead by Rock.

When you are able to say the words *my life flashed before my eyes*, you are not dead. You are alive. Because sometimes life is like a movie, and the twists are so unexpected, you never could have guessed they were even possible. Like when the person you think is the biggest idiot you've ever met turns out not to be an idiot at all. In fact, he turns out to be unbelievably resourceful and brave. And the imaginary friend of that brave not-idiot—the one who loves making the most improbable engineering projects—is very real. Gary Jr. and me discover all this the second Lance pops that lid.

The box explodes, blowing up in Lance's face in an eruption of glitter, a deafening siren, and pulsing strobe lights that toss him onto his back. The sound and light and madness do not stop. The glitter plume shoots into the night sky, blinding us as it rains down, blanketing the boat.

In the chaos, our leg zip ties are sliced, an arm hooks my arm, and another hooks Gary's arm. And we're guided up onto the Boston Whaler bench, then the rail, where Vaughn shouts, *"JUMP!"*

No time to think.

I prepare for the salty shock of cold and wet, but another

boat—*the* other boat—skids right at us, spraying water, close enough to Vaughn's boat to catch us, but not so close that it crashes.

We land in a pile on the floor. The engine revs high, and we're shot away from the chaos, away from Lance and Rock, and north toward the tip of Dolphin Point.

In the darkness, Vaughn guides us to the white-leather bench seats on the bow of...another Boston Whaler. We look back to the boat we'd just been on. The sound of the glitter bomb mixes with the siren of a police boat, blue lights flashing, zooming right at Lance and Rock, who are still fumbling around, trying to keep upright in the hurricane of glitter.

Gary lunges at Vaughn, trying to hug him with his zip-tied wrists. "Thank you, Vaughn. Thank you. Thank you."

Vaughn slices the zip ties, and we rub hands over sore wrists as he takes a seat on the bench across from us. He nods to the driver and shouts at us over the roar of the engine. "Guys! I'd like you to meet Charlie!"

She waves at us, beaming a massive, proud smile out of the hood of her puffy jacket.

"Her dad owns the Boston Whaler dealership in Poulsbo. That's how we got the boats."

"Wow!" Gary says. "Just *wow*!"

We skim over those dark Puget Sound waters, toward the dock. When we're close, Charlie quiets the engine and we slow to a crawl.

"What just happened?" Gary says. "When did you even plan this?"

"When they kidnapped me yesterday, Lance told me if I led them to the money they'd split it with me. I acted thrilled. I acted like I loved those guys and like I hated you. They believed me. They got cocky and I was able to slip away and sneak a quick phone call to Charlie this morning before I FaceTimed you guys. After that they took away my phone.

"Between then and now, Charlie rigged the glitter bomb and the crab pot and got us set up with the boats and tipped the cops off to what was happening. The boat was wired. They were listening to the whole thing."

Me and Gary cheer and chant, "Charlie! Charlie!"

Charlie takes a big bow. "My best glitter bomb so far! Not even close!"

Vaughn sits on the bench next to me. He holds a hand out to shake. I take his hand and pull that guy into a hug.

He starts crying. "I ruined the robbery. I got you put in prison. It was all my fault."

I pull out of the hug. "It's okay, man. I get it."

"Seriously?" he says.

"Hell yes. Fresh start?" I say, offering a hand again.

"Yeah," he says. "Fresh start." Vaughn wipes his snotty nose on the back of his sleeve. He laughs, saying, "Way to jump on Rock! Gary woulda sprung a leak if you hadn't done that."

"And what about this guy's two-footed kick?" I say, tapping Gary's chest.

"It was nothing," Gary says. "But it was awesome. And Vaughn, buddy, you did a great acting job back there. The anger and power when you slapped us? Oscar-worthy, my man. But I gotta come clean. Me completely losing my crap back there? I wasn't acting. That was totally real. Hundred percent."

"Serious?" Vaughn says.

"Swear to God," Gary says. He watches me check the time. "Oh no, guys! Tonio has to make his meeting!"

I ask Vaughn if he thinks Charlie could get us back to the Des Moines Marina.

He says he'd love to give us a ride back but Charlie's dad isn't thrilled with all this. He wants her and the boat back ASAP. "There's a five-twenty ferry to Fauntleroy." He turns to Charlie. "How long is the crossing?"

"Half hour," she says. "About that."

"But, guys," Gary says, "if Tonio misses this meeting—"

"It's okay," I say. "We'll take the ferry. It's all right."

It's a thirty-minute drive to Des Moines from Fauntleroy in West Seattle. *If Claudio can pick us up, and if there's no traffic…*

If we can convince him to go to the marina, and if, by some miracle, the shovel stayed stuck in the mud and the cord held and the bags haven't floated away, me and Gary will grab them, and we'll stash the money in my mom's studio. I'll change clothes and we'll zip over to Puget High—*please, dear God*—on time for my meeting.

Vaughn can come over after school gets out, and he and Gary and I can split the money.

And I'll begin the process of making amends with my mom by handing her thousands of dollars and taking away a mountain of financial stress that's built up for years, and putting her and Claudio in a position to have the home they need.

I reach my hand into my pocket to grab my phone and send the text. It's still sticky from the beer spill. *Beer spill. Oh no! Nancy's car!*

That's when I see the missed notifications. The first is a text from Claudio.

> Waiting for you at Donuts.
> Where are you? Please tell me you are ok

There are more like that. And a bunch of texts directly from my mom. Which means Claudio told her we switched phones. Her messages break my heart so much, I can't get through them. Plus, I need to fill Claudio in on my current situation.

> Hi Claudio! I am alive. Yay! How are you? I hope you're doing great. Sorry 4 not showing up. Life got very crazy.

> Anyways no need to ask me ?s right now...super-long stories for another time lol. 🙂

> My dad's # is in my contacts. Text him please and tell him the Miata is across the street from the marina pier parking lot. 🙇

And could you please pick me up this morn @ Fauntleroy ferry @ 6am sharp. 🙏

Lastly, please do not tell my mom those two requests but do tell her I'm going to be on time to my meeting and looking forward to seeing her and . . . big hug?

Also, Claudio, you are the best thing that ever happened to this family. 🖤 🥺

Claudio's response comes fast.

Processing . . . . WTF!?!?!

Will text ur dad re (borrowed? stolen?) car.

Will pick you up @ ferry. But no more secrets btwn me & your mom. EVER.

Lastly. I am happy you're alive because I am strongly considering killing you. 🖤 🥺

If ur mom doesn't kill us both first.

Charlie lands us at a public park dock. She apologizes that there's no good place to drop us off closer. We can see the ferry terminal from here, but it's gonna be a long walk.

We thank her for saving our lives. As brilliant as Charlie is, she turns to Vaughn like she believes he's the amazing one. "This was Vaughn's idea. His plan. I just had to make it happen."

"Wow, Vaughn," Gary says, "I underestimated you. And for that, I am sorry."

"Your friend took a big risk to make this happen," Charlie says. "For you."

Vaughn shrugs, his face turning red.

"And that crab!" she says. "That was my signal to come at you guys hard and fast. Awesome touch, huh? Again, totally Vaughn's idea."

Vaughn sucks on a finger and shakes it in the air. "That thing hurt for real."

"Same with you slapping me," Gary says. "The pain I felt was like you were actually *trying* to hurt me. Again, a top-notch performance, Vaughn."

"I needed to convince them I was actually mad at you guys and that I was on their side."

"It worked," Gary says.

"And the truth is, I was mad at you. My lawyer played a cell phone recording of you two planning the robbery. You called me *idiot* a bunch of times. You both talked like that was my actual name."

We tell him how sorry we are.

"We're even now," he says.

"Yeah," I say. "We are."

"Not so fast," Gary says. "We still gotta dig up that money and split it three ways. Just like we always planned."

Vaughn shakes his head. "When Rock and Lance kidnapped me, I had just moved back. I got a job lined up at Charlie's dad's dealership." He and Charlie smile big at each other. "It pays well. They're setting me up with a little studio apartment close to work. So I'm good. Seriously, you guys, I don't want to touch that drug money ever again."

Drug money. Damn.

"Too much pain," he says. "Too many bad vibes." Vaughn reaches out his hand one last time.

I shake it, nodding at him, still trying to tell him I got no bad feelings left, hoping he doesn't either.

"Vaughn?" Gary says. "The irony is, me and Tonio are strapped. You got ferry money?"

Charlie pulls out a wallet and hands us a twenty. "Good luck, you two."

"Good luck, guys," Gary says.

We watch Vaughn and Charlie in the moonlight as they slowly make their way toward Vashon's northwest point. They're shoulder to shoulder, his arm wrapped around her waist as she steers the Whaler. They'll sail north on this Puget Sound stretch of the Salish Sea, between the west coast of Bainbridge Island and the shores of Kitsap Peninsula, all the way up to Poulsbo. And I bet they go like that the whole way, shoulder to shoulder, his arm around her back, the sun rising on them, blessing this morning, blessing Vaughn and Charlie as they sail into their future.

Maya and me were not meant to be.

I think Vaughn and Charlie are meant to be. I hope they are.

"Charlie is real," Gary says. "They are a girl. A beautiful and tough and brilliant woman with a cherry Boston Whaler. And she loves *Vaughn*."

"Yup," I say, teeth chattering as a wave of wet cold finally takes over my whole body.

"We're the idiots," Gary says.

"Yup," I say.

"Let's walk, Tonio. That'll warm you up."

We make our way through the park, then along the shoulder of Vashon Highway until we're on a sidewalk, under streetlights, walking through town. In a few minutes we're sitting on a bench outside the tiny yellow ferry terminal, waiting for five o'clock, when the doors will open and we can buy our tickets.

"I'm really tired," Gary says, his head falling toward my shoulder.

"Uh-uh," I say. "If you knock out, I will too. We can't risk missing this boat. If we do, I'm screwed. Talk to me, Gary. Keep me awake."

"I don't have a story, Tonio. You talk."

When I Promised to Change

So then... Grace drove me to school
on the first day after the end of my suspension.

She shook hands with Mrs. Lucrisia and Mr. Matthews.

He asked how we were related.

I told him Grace had given me a job and a place to stay.

She gave them her number, winked, and said,

> You call me from now on.

We made a plan for success—
check-ins with Mrs. Lucrisia and the social worker,
a sober-support program, and weekly reports from teachers.

I signed the papers. And said goodbye to Grace.

• • •

In Orton's math class, I was lost cuz of all the days I'd missed.

But I promised myself I would not get down.
I would raise my hand, ask questions,
stay after class, and study for hours,
cuz I had to make this work.

Just as I made those promises,
Mr. Matthews opened the door,
and he called me into the hall,
where I was met by two county cops
who cuffed me, threw me in a van,
and drove me away to Seattle,
where I spent days in juvie lockup. Juvie school.
Back and forth to juvie court.
But mostly, juvie was endless waiting.
Waiting and waiting for days and days.
Waiting to learn my fate.

MONDAY 5:05 AM

We walk aboard the *Kittitas*. It's huge for a boat. Medium-size for a Washington State ferry. If you walk on, it's hard to get to work from the Fauntleroy ferry terminal without a long bus ride. So most commuters drive on. There are a bunch of cars already loaded up because this boat originates at Southworth, just west of here on the Kitsap Peninsula. Everyone is headed to work at Amazon in Seattle, or at Boeing—the factory over in Renton or the one up in Everett. Probably some people headed out to Microsoft in Redmond.

Out of the hundreds of people on this boat, I'm guessing that today, me and Gary are the only ones who might end up getting their hands on more cash than most people will touch in their lives. And I'm guessing I'm the only one who has a chance of ending this day in prison.

Gary and I get the strangest looks from these people, all uptight in their fancy, sharp business suits and their soft, hipster-casual business suits, and their REI gear. They've never seen a couple teenagers on a boat before?

We head outside to the rear deck. The wind is whipping. It's freezing. We lean over the rail and watch black water churn into white froth as the engine kicks to life, and slowly, slowly, the boat separates from the shadow that is Vashon.

Gary Jr. points to the sunrise above the Olympic Mountains, too soon threatening to turn night into day. "Isn't it ironic?" he says. "We're in the biggest hurry of our lives. And we're on the slowest possible form of transportation known to man."

"Can we change the subject?"

"I bet you are *freaking* out. I would totally be freaking."

"Yeah. I am. Okay?"

"I got weed."

"None for me. But you go ahead. We keep facing this way, no one will see you."

Gary pulls out a baggie. A blunt. Gets it lit up.

I clear my throat and take in a big deep breath cuz I'm gonna get real with Gary. "So..."

"You sure you don't want some?"

"Still on parole." I say that like I haven't broken a million terms already.

"Right," Gary says. "I'm sorry I been pushy on that, Tonio."

The apology comes out so sincere. And the look on this kid's face. Open. Loving. Sad. I have to come clean. "Gary, are you still curious why I was on the beach instead of meeting you at the gate?"

He lets out a steady stream of smoke and opens his eyes. "I was trying to not think about it. That didn't work. So I been imagining it was related to you having the very best intentions. Like when you attacked Rock to save my life."

"Then you kicked his gun away to save mine."

"I finally saved your life, Tonio. Feels pretty good."

"Me being at the marina before you got there wasn't that kind of good."

Gary takes a deep hit.

"My dad told me Lance and Rock were chasing Vaughn. When Vaughn said that stuff about meeting him in a boat, I knew they had him. I went to the marina early because I didn't want Lance to end up with the money."

"What about me?" he says.

"Honestly?"

"Honestly."

"I wasn't thinking about it."

"It?"

"You."

Gary flashes me watery eyes and a sorry face as his head collapses onto the rail. He just stays there, bent over like that for a long time.

"I didn't want them to get it. I didn't want to have to deal with drama. And I wanted that money for my mom. She's got massive hospital bills to pay. I thought I could go early and get away with those bags."

Gary lifts his head and stands up straight. "Did you dig them up?"

"They're floating in the water just north of the pier. Anchored by a shovel. You and me are gonna go get them and split the money fifty-fifty."

Gary releases smoke in a slow, steady stream. When the smoke clears, he smiles that Gary smile that says, *I'm forgiving you. Again. I'm still here. Still by your side.* He points toward Seattle and says, "Then you and me are headed for that condo, right?"

"I'm gonna try to live with my mom," I say. "I'm hoping the money will make a difference for us."

"I hope it does too."

"I had thought it might make a difference for Maya too."

"Yeah?"

"But we talked, and I realized it's not our job to take care of each other anymore."

Gary puts an arm around my shoulders. "You okay with that, Tonio?"

"I will be."

"That's good."

"We said goodbye."

"*Goodbye* goodbye? Like not even hanging out?"

"Yeah. That kind of goodbye."

"Sorry, man," Gary says. "But"—he looks at me full of hope—"maybe someday?"

"We have to get to know ourselves first. We have to live our lives like there's no *maybe someday.*"

"I don't like it," Gary says, "but I get it."

"I said goodbye to my dad too."

"That's good," he says. "I mean, you good with that, Tonio?"

"I'm good with it," I say. And that's the truth. But it doesn't hurt any less.

"And we both said goodbye to Vaughn. Cuz he's got his new life. I don't think we'll ever see that kid again."

"Him saying let's start over, that was a polite *goodbye* goodbye."

"What do you think about that, Tonio?"

"Him starting fresh is a good thing. What do *you* think?"

"It's good. But when someone starts fresh without you, that's sad. But it's like you and Maya, I guess. Sometimes you gotta say goodbye so a fresh start can happen."

"Yeah," I say. "You do."

Gary straightens up tall, his puppy-dog eyes welling because he's gonna ask me the question I'm still not ready for. The one about *us*. "That's a lot of goodbyes, Tonio. You think—" But the question is interrupted. "Look!" he shouts, throwing his arm out over the rail, pointing.

I try to track his finger. But everything just looks dark.

"Out there!" he says.

I can't see it.

"That band of moonlight on the water. Follow my finger. Keep your eyes on that spot."

I finally see them. Black, towering dorsal fins. Arched backs surfacing and submerging. *Orcas.*

"J Pod." Gary says it like he's just seen God.

There might be twenty in the pod. But only a couple surface at a time. Whenever I lose them, Gary Jr. points and gets them back for me.

"You hear about that mama?" he says.

"What mama?"

"You missed a lot while you were in there."

"That's for sure."

"There was this J Pod orca cow. She's probably swimming out

there right now," he says, pointing at them again. "Her calf died right after it was born. But the cow wouldn't let her baby sink to the bottom. She kept pushing it to the top of the water with her nose, keeping it up on the surface."

"Jesus. For how long?"

"They followed her swimming like that with her baby for seventeen days."

"What?"

"A thousand miles!"

"Was she hoping it would come to life?"

"They said it was grief. Me and Maya talked about it one of those times at Westernco. Maya thought she was mourning her baby. Whatever she was doing, that mama just didn't want to let her baby go. I wonder if, when she finally did, it was because she was ready or because she was so tired."

"That's the saddest thing I've ever heard."

"Sad the calf died. But the mama doing that...I think it's amazing. It's beautiful."

"Yeah?"

"If she'd have let her calf go when she realized it was dead, no one would have said a thing. A story about an orca calf dying would have come and gone fast. The way the mama chose to do it...people were glued to that story. Reporters started throwing out facts and figures about the disappearing orca, and people were like, *What is up with our Puget Sound whales?*"

"You think she did it for people?"

"It was grief *and* it was a protest. Me and Maya both thought that. The mama was like, *Look at what you've done!* Forcing us all to look and to think about what we've done to the rivers and Lake Washington and the Sound and the Salish Sea and the Pacific—all the places that used to provide orcas their salmon before we came around. She was grieving her baby...and fighting for a decent place to raise future babies. That's what me and Maya think."

As we pass the pod, one huge orca breaches, nose to the sky, then tosses back with a massive splash. It's awesome. *Awesome.*

"Isn't life surprising?" Gary says. "That's what makes it worth it."

Gary stares at that swath of moonlight on the water like something else amazing could happen at any moment.

"Hey, man," I say.

"Yeah?"

"You know you said your movie was going to be the story of our lives?"

"Uh-huh."

"I think there's a lot of stuff I never told you about me."

"And you're going to tell me that stuff?"

"Yeah. But I think there's a lot of stuff I don't know about you. Maybe you could—"

"That's a good trade," he says. Then he pulls his baggie out of his pocket. He opens it, raises it out over the railing. He shakes the baggie, and the weed is carried away in the wind.

"What's up with that?" I say.

"I told you I needed Final Draft to write my script. That's an excuse. I could write a script without it. But every time I start writing, something stops me. Something I can't get past."

"What stops you?"

"I don't know. But I do know that when I get stuck like that, I smoke a ton of weed. *A ton*, Tonio. I'm thinking if I don't have weed, maybe I'll sit there with my hands on the keyboard until I get past whatever it is." He looks out to the water. "Maybe I'm already past it."

"Really?"

"Yeah."

"That's cool, Gary."

• • •

The boat approaches the dock, and the engines start pushing in reverse to slow the beast down.

I check my phone. 5:50.

I close my eyes.

I inhale deep.

Before I can exhale, Gary nudges my arm. "We gotta go."

We take off running across the deck, into the cabin, past rows and rows of bench seats, down the stairwell, and into the front of the walkers' line.

I search the crowd of people waiting for friends or loved ones. Claudio is not there.

My mom is.

MONDAY 5:55 AM

Lit up by dawn and by a yellow-white flood of fluorescent light, my mom looks like a wreck. Her jaw drops when she sees us. She launches herself onto me. Squeezing me so damn tight. So tight, I can feel her breathing. Gasping. She's crying. She lets go of me, wipes her eyes with her sleeve. She reaches out a hand to touch my face. "¿Qué es eso?"

"What is what?"

"It's all over your clothes."

"Glitter," Gary says. "It stuck to him good."

"*Glitter?* You smell like beer. What kind of a party—?"

"Beer? I haven't—" The glitter stuck to the beer my dad spilled on me.

"Sorry to break up this touching reunion, but we really gotta get to Tonio's meeting!"

My mom glares at Gary, then turns and walks.

We follow. I want to explain this night. I don't know how.

We pile into the Subaru. Me in the front. Gary in back.

She starts the engine. Backs up. Drives to the entrance. We have to wait for cars streaming off the boat before we can turn onto Fauntleroy Way.

Someone finally lets us in. And we're on our way to Des Moines.

I pray she'll take us to the marina.

I pray the money's there and we can get it fast enough.

I pray we make it to my meeting on time.

"Antonio?" she says.

I turn to her.

Her hands grip the wheel tight. "No podemos vivir así."

"*We* can't live like this?" I say. "*I* can't live like this. I don't want to go through another weekend like this one, ever."

She shakes her head like she's got more to say to me but she can't get it out.

"Stuff happened, Mamá. Stuff I didn't know I had to deal with. Stuff I was afraid of. I'm not afraid of anything now." Then it erupts from my guts and my heart and shoots out my mouth before I can stop it: "Except you."

Her head whips my way. Her jaw drops again. "Me?"

"You think I'm him."

And the rest comes out in a waterfall of crying words. Her words cascading over my words. Us finally saying what we need to.

"Him *who*?" she says.

"Dad."

"*Dad? What?* No es cierto."

"The way you looked at me, Mamá. That's why I ran."

"What are you—"

"Just like at Tammy's. Before I got arrested. When you sent me away."

"That was her. *She* sent you away."

"Oh, *come on, Mamá*! I needed you!"

"You were drunk. You were scary."

"I was running from Dad. I needed you. I needed a home. That look on your face. You turned me away."

She's crying, wiping her eyes, sniffling, trying to watch the traffic. When she can finally get words out, she says, "I was sick, mijo. I wasn't sleeping. I was exhausted. *I* was running away from him too. No podía..."

"You couldn't *what*?"

"Everything. Anything. I couldn't. I didn't know how. Mijo, lo siento. I failed. Lo siento. Forgive me."

I want to, but I can't get the words out.

"I'm here now," she says. "I'm trying now. I'm not going to ever stop trying. Because I need you. I love you. I have a home for you. I need you and your sister together." She reaches her hand to mine. Grabs it strong. Squeezes so hard.

I feel it.

"I wasn't the mother you deserved. I hurt you. I need you to forgive me."

"What else?"

She nods, eyes on the road. Sniffs. Wipes her face with her sleeve again. "I need you to sleep in your bed. I need you to be honest with me and Claudio. I need you to stay out of trouble. I need you to stay away from your dad."

"And you need money for your hospital bills?"

"*What?*"

"Money for Claudio's addition?"

"Mijo, what are you talking—"

"I can get that money. It's waiting for us at the marina. Money to take care of everything. Dad gave up. He left you high and dry. Stuck you with all that debt. I'm not him. I won't do that."

"Is this why you been out all night?"

"You need money. I saw the bill. You said it. Claudio said it. I'm going to take care of you."

"That's not your job. I don't need you to—"

"What *do* you need?"

"I told you! I need a chance. I need to be your mamá. I need you to trust me. To trust that I can take care of you. *Let me.*"

It's quiet for a while.

I feel a poke on my shoulder. I turn back. Gary has tears rolling down his face. He silently points at my mom's back and mouths the words *For. . . give . . . her!*

"I'm a different person than I was at Tammy's," she says. "I'm healthy. I can think straight. I have Olivia. I have Claudio. I am almost happy. All I want . . . all I need . . . is you."

"All I need is you, Mamá. I forgive you. Can you forgive me? For all the crap I pulled?"

"Sí, mijo. ¡Soy tu mamá! Now you better explain why you smell like beer and why you're covered in mud and glitter."

I explain to my mom what happened over the weekend. When the story gets crazy, Gary pipes in. "It's true. That really happened, Ms. Echeverría."

I tell my mom about my goodbyes. Goodbye to Maya. Goodbye to my dad. I tell her about my year and a half of desperation at Zephyr, wanting to know where I stood with Maya, and where I stood with her.

I'm not proud of how I acted with Maya this weekend. If I could take all that back, I would. And it was stupid to see my dad. But there was stuff I needed to know. And now I know.

I tell her about the Sharpie I stole. I tell her I hit my dad. I tell her about taking Nancy's car to the marina. I tell her about the money. About Lance. Rock. Vaughn.

I tell her it's all behind me. And I'm ready now to start my new life.

She says she can't take one cent of that money. "We're going to be okay, mijo. We're going to make it. We're on a payment plan. We have a lawyer. We're negotiating that bill down. We're going to be okay. I need you to trust that. I need you to trust us."

I sit with that. And my whole plan feels stupid now. Like more desperation. And in the quiet of our drive, I feel it. Something else. One last thing gnawing inside me. There's something else I have to make right. One more person I need to forgive.

The person I need to make amends to.

And I know exactly how.

I tell my mom what that is. I know it sounds crazy. I tell her why I have to do it.

She says it can wait.

I tell her it can't.

"Okay, mijo." She takes a deep breath. "Okay."

Gary pipes in from the back seat. "I'm doing it too, Tonio."

I tell him he doesn't have to.

He tells me he does.

I tell him I won't let him.

He says I'm not the boss of his life.

I check the time.

Gary nods his head, resolute. "We got time, Tonio," he says. "We can do this."

I make the call to Claudio.

The car tires squeal as we make the turn into the marina parking lot.

"Wait right here with the hatch up," I say. "We'll be right back."

My mom slams on the brakes.

We explode out of the car, sprint through the parking lot to the second lamppost, and hop the rail.

I spot the bags floating far up the beach, the tide having pulled up the shovel and dragged it. We run as fast as we can, knowing that when we get there, we won't be able to just wade in. The bags are too far out.

We shed layers, running, hopping, to the edge of the water. Forlán gone. Hoodie gone. T-shirt gone. Shoes and jeans gone. Gary shouts, "*Polar bear plunge!*" and we sprint-splash into the freezing water, diving headfirst, submerging ourselves in a silent green world of freezing cold and seaweed and salt. We are a part of our Puget Sound. And we are alive.

We drag the bags onto the shore and get dressed, pulling dry clothes over wet bodies. Gary Jr. slips on pants, shivering the words "To-d-d-d-day. You-you-you and-me-me-me, we were-were-were-were EPIC TO-TO-TO-TOGETHER, T-t-t-t-onio!"

Claudio is standing out in front of Haven. Olivia is in his arms.

My mom pops the trunk.

Gary and I rush around to grab the bags.

My mom heads off with Olivia.

Claudio has the keys to the front door, but he says we shouldn't put the bags inside. He takes us around back. There's a tall fence around the trash containers, and a locked gate. "Pickup isn't till Friday. Toss them over the gate. Carol is the manager today. She'll be in first. Write her a note. Drop it in the mailbox. She'll get it."

Gary Jr. climbs the chain-link. "Up here," he says. "Hand a bag to me."

I hand him the bag. He holds on. I climb up to join him, then we hoist that thing over together. Claudio hands us the second bag, and we do it again. Gary jumps over and stuffs the bags in the bin.

Then I grab a piece of paper and a pen from Claudio.

I'm stuck looking at him. Imagining the face of the guy he

was. Thinking about the kid I was. I'm crying again and I can't get myself together to write this note.

Claudio grabs me. Bear-hugs me. Pats my back. "It's okay now," he says. "It's over."

I don't stop crying. Don't break out of his hug.

"Come on!" Gary says. "We have to get you to school."

I silently plead with Claudio to say it, to forgive me.

"Uh-uh," he says. "I tried already. This one's yours."

I close my eyes. And in my mind, I say the words I need to hear.

You were a kid. You were afraid. You were doing your best under the worst circumstances, at the worst possible time of your life. So you made every bad choice. But you survived. And it's time to move on. I forgive you, Antonio. I forgive you. I forgive you.

I grab the pen and write fast.

> Dear Carol,
> Check the trash for two dry bags.
> The money inside was taken from a
> local dealer. It came from people
> addicted to opioids. This is THEIR
> MONEY. Use it to help them.

When a Period of Waiting Finally Ended and Another One Just Got Started

So then it came, a new deal I couldn't refuse.

I was cuffed and shackled in the back of a van,
headed for two years of incarceration in a
little prison in a forest on the Olympic Peninsula...

Zephyr Woods Youth Detention Center.

Somewhere on that drive, the part of my mind that's
capable of imagining, hoping, believing, loving...
was sucked out of me. And into that void
flooded a torrent of rage.

Getting me inside that place would be no breeze.
I fought drivers and guards, writhing, kicking, screaming,
fighting in order to flee...
to get back to my mom, to get back to Maya,
to get back to Grace, to get back to the pier,
to get back to myself, to get back to my mind.

In a padded room, wrapped tight in that jacket,
I knew I'd lost, all was lost, no going back,
but the rage wasn't gone,
so I fought the floor and the walls.
I fought and I fought and I fought and I fought...

MONDAY `6:52 AM`

Gary and me end up in the back seat together. Claudio is going as fast as he can down 24th when he looks into the rearview mirror. He shakes his head, saying, "No time to get you cleaned up." He reaches over to the glove compartment, pulls out a rag, and tosses it into the back seat.

I do my best. But stuff is stuck on me like glue. I'm wet. I'm muddy. I smell. But if I can make it to my meeting on time, and if Murdock overlooks the mess I am...

I lean over to catch a look in the rearview mirror.

Jesus.

My hands start shaking.

My legs start shaking.

My face is tingling.

And if Murdock can overlook me seeing my dad and hitting him, and stealing Nancy's car, which he'll know if she called the cops. Cuz why wouldn't she call the cops?

My breath runs away from me.

I can't—I can't—I can't—

I try.

To slow.

But I can't.

Cuz I don't.

Can't.

Go back.

To Zephyr.

I need to be here.

With my mom.

My sister.

Grace.

I need to be in school.

Here.

I can't go back there.

Breathe.

I can't.

Breathe, Antonio!

I can't.

I can't catch my—

We're approaching the turn onto 223rd. Just minutes away.

The doors of this car are closing in on me. And there's

only one

thing to—

My fingers grip the door handle. To open up—

to jump—

to run—

But something—

A touch.

Skin.

On my skin.

Warmth from the palm of a hand.

On the back of my hand.

My eyes drop.

Gary's Jr.'s hand is resting on my hand.

Gary's Jr.'s skin on my skin.

I look up at him.

His eyes are closed.

He inhales as long, as deep, as he can.

Eyes still closed, he exhales as long and slow as he can.

He inhales deep again.

Exhales slow again.

And without even thinking, I try.

My inhale is a short, desperate gulp.

I feel myself holding my breath, waiting for Gary's exhale.

I exhale with him, pushing as long as I can.

I close my eyes, waiting for his breath. Exhaling when he does. Inhaling when he does.

I keep going like that. Chasing Gary's breath. Until we're together.

Inhaling deep.

Exhaling slow.

My hand falls from the door handle.

We inhale deep.

Exhale slow.

Inhale deep.

Exhale slow.

When I Learned How to Breathe

So then, in the padded room, I'm on the floor,
my back pressed stiff against the wall,
my fists balled, muscles flexed, one knee pumping
up and down, up and down, up and down.

I was
exhausted
but
could
not
stop
my
breath
from—

The door opened.
In walked a lady who looked like a grandmother.
She stood there as the door closed behind her.

> *Oh, sweet boy, she said. It's been a rough day.*
> *I came to sit with you.*

I heard the
words
but I
couldn't—
I couldn't—
I couldn't—

Nod your head if you can hear me.

I nodded to the lady.

May I sit with you?

I nodded to the lady.

She sat down in her nice clothes
on the padded floor with me.
And she rested a palm on my hand.

I looked at her face. Her eyes were closed.
I watched for them to open.
But they didn't.
I listened for her to speak more words.
But she didn't.

She just slowly breathed in...

...and slowly breathed out.

322

Over and over.

No words.

Just breathing.

No words.

Just breath.

No words.

Until . . .

I don't know when. But at some point it started.
I was breathing right along with that lady.

• • •

She opened her eyes.
I sensed it and opened mine.

> *Hello, Antonio. I'm Mrs. Williams.*

I nodded to Mrs. Williams.

> *When you are overstressed, anxious, agitated, terrified,*
> *that shallow, short breathing and your mind screaming to fight*
> > *or run*

are nature's way of preparing you to act in the face of danger.

But nature doesn't know the difference
between the times you truly need to fight or run
and the times you'd be better off
taking a moment to calm yourself,
quiet your mind, and think things through.

Those are the moments when we need to

inhale deep

then

exhale slow and long.

Good. Shall we do it again?

I nodded to Mrs. Williams.

She closed her eyes.

I closed mine.

We inhaled deep.

We exhaled slow.

And sat doing nothing but that for the longest time.

We inhale deep.

We exhale slow.

Inhale deep.

Exhale slow.

Inhale deep.

I'm gonna face the music.

Exhale slow.

I'm going in there.

Inhale deep.

I'm gonna tell my story.

Exhale slow.

I feel Gary's hand lift off of mine.

I open my eyes.

"Wow, Tonio," he says, "that is some seriously powerful shit."

"Oxygen?"

"Oh yeah."

"Right?" I say. "I been trying to do that all weekend."

"Your weekend has been too much to even breathe."

"Tell me about it."

"Tonio," he says, "now that your head is clear, we gotta get something straight between us. And we gotta do it now, because in a minute you'll be running into your meeting."

"What, Gary?"

He looks out the window as we make a right onto 223rd, just one block to the turn into the Puget High parking lot. "You said a lot of goodbyes this weekend. Like, for-real, forever goodbyes."

"Yeah," I say.

"You got another of those goodbyes left to say? Cuz if you do, you better do it now."

I think about the goodbyes.

Maya. Fighting to hang on to the old Maya, the *old us*…that felt like desperation.

Vaughn. Hanging on to hating him felt a lot like hating myself.

My dad. Hanging on to the idea that we could have a future… that felt like hanging on to a life of fear and endless disappointment.

My mom. I'm hanging on tight to her. But letting the resentment go.

The only thing worse than hanging on to resentment of my mom was hanging on to the stuff I felt about myself.

I'm happy to say goodbye to all of it.

But Gary Jr.?

I look right at him. Those eyes. His smile.

Holding on to Gary means believing in the possibility that

there is goodness in the world. There is true friendship. Endless curiosity. Endless hope. And a person to breathe with.

"*Goodbye* goodbye was the plan when I went to see you at Westernco. It was the plan after the party. It was the plan after I left your apartment yesterday. It was the plan on the beach before I saw you on the pier last night."

"We've been through a lot since then, Tonio."

"Yeah we have."

"So?"

"So I'm never going to treat you like that again. I swear, Gary. I'm sorry I ever did. And I promise you I'm gonna be the kind of friend you deserve from here on out, because you are stuck with me for the long haul."

"That's good. Because you know you're stuck with me. For the long haul." He unbuckles his seat belt and lunges onto me. He squeezes me around the shoulders tight as he can. "Damn universe has a way, Tonio. It has a way." Then he drops back into his seat, smiling.

Approaching the turn into the school drop-off, we get stuck behind buses backed up all the way out into the street. "You gotta get outta here," Claudio says. "And run!"

"Let's go, Tonio!" Gary jumps out and starts running.

I hop out and pump my arms and legs right behind him as he clears a path through the crowd of kids.

"Comin' through!" Gary shouts.

They throw us wild-eyed looks.

Gary pushes through. "Make way for Tonio!"

Fifty yards to go.

Twenty-five.

Ten.

I pull open the front door and run past the office entrance, around the corner to the conference-room door.

Before I open it, Gary Jr. grabs me by the shoulders. "You got this, Tonio! You hear me? You got this!"

I walk in with Gary Jr. I make eye contact with my mom, who is sitting at the conference-room table, holding Olivia on her shoulder. Grace is here too! And she brought Tommy. They closed Westernco Donut for this! Mr. Matthews is here. All these people to support me in my transition back.

"Oh, Antonio," Mrs. Lucrisia says.

"Um . . . *wow*," Murdock says.

Their jaws hang. Their eyes are wide open. They're staring at me like this situation is one for the books.

"This is going to be quick," Murdock says. He stands and positions himself next to me, his back firm against the door. He introduces himself to everyone. Then he says how disappointed he is.

As expected, Nancy had called the cops about me taking the car and about hitting my dad. Apparently, my dad already talked her into not pressing charges.

"Charges or no charges," Murdock says, "you broke the law.

You broke curfew. You made contact with your father. It's obvious you've been drinking. That's four broken terms right there."

"I didn't drink," I say.

"You were out of touch for long periods of time. That's five." He looks at Gary Jr. "And your friend is on probation."

"I didn't know you couldn't—" Gary says his face turning red.

I smile at him. To let him know it's okay. Cuz I needed him this weekend. And I'm going to need him moving forward.

"You were late to this meeting."

"Like three minutes."

"Six conditions of parole violated. In three days. Might be a record."

"If you'd just let me—"

"Transitions back are difficult," he says. "This is why there are parole conditions to begin with. I hate to do it, Antonio, but this one's an easy call."

There's a knock on the door. Officer Murdock opens it. Claudio enters and takes a seat.

Murdock reaches for his belt. "I'll phone the squad car to transport you back to Juvenile Court in Seattle. There'll be a short hearing. Then a trip back to Zephyr Woods."

He unclips handcuffs from his belt and turns to me. "Sorry, man. Hands behind your back."

"Please," I beg, "let me explain."

Murdock says he doesn't know what I could possibly say.

"He said he can explain!" my mom says. "Let him!"

"Let the boy talk!" Grace says.

Gary and Claudio chime in too.

Murdock looks to Mr. Matthews and Mrs. Lucrisia like he's asking them to quiet things down.

They're looking at him like he's the one who should do something.

Finally, Mrs. Lucrisia puts two fingers between her teeth and whistles loud.

The room falls silent.

"Antonio," Mrs. Lucrisia says, "I'm looking at you and you are a mess, which is the understatement of the year. You knew this was a school day. You knew you'd be attending this important meeting. You knew you'd see Officer Murdock. I know you well enough to believe there's no way you'd be here looking like this unless something happened to you. Something big. I want to hear what it was."

I turn to Murdock. Everyone in the room does.

"This meeting was set to go an hour," Mrs. Lucrisia says.

Murdock checks his watch. He lets out a big, tired breath and turns to me. "All right, man. Let's hear it. But we all know where this is headed."

I nod.

I swallow.

I open my eyes and scan the room.

I make eye contact with Mr. Matthews. Mrs. Lucrisia. Grace and Tommy. Claudio. My mom. Olivia. And Gary Jr. He gives me a thumbs-up, his iPhone at his chest, where only I can see the video light is on. He's catching all this. Because he's really gonna make that film of our lives someday. And he's gonna have to remember what happened.

There's a buzz in my pocket.

A text from Maya.

"Hold on a sec," I say. "I promise." I click the text. A GIF opens up.

Our great blue heron at the pier at sunset.

Her beak pointed upward.

Wings slowly unfolding.

Downward pushing.

Upward lifting.

Taking flight.

Then a text.

Make a wish!

I could make my wish for this moment. But I make one for someday.

I wished! You?

I wished you all the wishes.

I set my phone on the table and send Maya a mental message of thanks for not giving up on me.

My phone buzzes again.

All the best, Antonio! And keep your eye on the water. (🦆 🐦 🗽)

I send silent thank-yous to my team from Zephyr. Charlie and Maureen from AA, Ms. Duncan, and Mrs. Williams.

I touch the shield on my heart. And I look up toward heaven, taking in one more big, deep breath, letting it fill me up with the goodness of all the people who have ever loved me.

No more raging.

No more fighting.

No more running.

I am calm.

"I know this looks really bad," I say. "*I* look really bad. But if you get past looks, and you listen to what's inside of me, you'll realize I'm more prepared to live my best life—a good, honest, productive, law-abiding, healthy life—than I ever have been.

"And that's not because of Zephyr Woods. Okay, there were a few people there who helped me a lot. *A lot.* And they got me part of the way. But mostly, the Zephyr experience was just incarceration. Depressing. Cold. Boring. Degrading. What prepared me the rest of the way was getting reacquainted with the people in this room—and getting to know a couple of them for the very first time. But that's not everything that prepared me. Believe it or not, it's the wildest stuff that happened to me this weekend that got me ready too. Yup. I'm prepared to live my best life because of everything that made me the mess who is standing before you today."

I remind myself to just tell my story. The whole story of the seventy-two hours after my release from prison. And no matter what happens with those handcuffs after my story is over, I know I did what I needed to do. I said the goodbyes I needed to say. I forgave the people I needed to forgive.

And in my mind, and in my heart, I am free.

AUTHOR'S NOTE

No Going Back is the last of a three-book cycle set in South King County in western Washington State (the other books are *American Road Trip* and *Jumped In*). The crime at the heart of *No Going Back* was inspired by an article about a young woman who spent time in a youth prison in Washington after setting up her friends to rob her father's drug supplier in order to feed herself and her siblings. I wanted to set the book in Washington, my home state, where, for a short time in the 1990s, I worked teaching drama to kids in a setting very similar to the fictional Zephyr Woods. However, in an effort to create a compelling story that reflected incarceration, sentencing, probation, and parole nationally, there are details in this fictional work that are not specific to youth detention and the juvenile justice system in Washington State, where, for example, AA is not used as a mandated intervention due to separation of church and state, and sentences for teens who've committed non-violent crimes are getting shorter.

ACKNOWLEDGMENTS

It takes a big crew to shepherd a book from initial inspiration all the way to publication. I owe the following folks more than thank-yous. Nevertheless, a huge thanks to agent Steven Chudney for helping me transition *No Going Back* from a seemingly never-ending series of experiments to a novel. Thanks to publisher-editor extraordinaire Christy Ottaviano for falling for the messy versions of Antonio—and Sam, Luis, and Teodoro—and for pushing all the right buttons in guiding me to realize their potential. Thanks to Jessica Anderson for years of work on my behalf at Christy Ottaviano Books.

Thanks to cover artist Adams Carvalho, art director Karina Granda, assistant editor Leyla Erkan, production editor Esther Reisberg, copy editor Lara Stelmaszyk, and proofreaders Tara Rayers and Daniel Lupo. And to the folks at Little, Brown Books for Young Readers and Hachette whose efforts and care helped bring this book to life.

Thank you to the readers of *No Going Back* manuscripts: Donte Felder, Vincent Delaney, Kirsten Heiken, Doug Kasischke, Heather Shumaker, Charlie Scott, Cristián Uriostegui, and Brandon Will. Your insights, questions, suggestions, and encouragement were invaluable. Thanks to Jeff Kass for letting me try out early ideas in his creative writing classes at Pioneer High School. Thanks to my Ann Arbor critique group; to accountability pals, Kristen Lenz and Katherine Higgs-Coulthard; and to my *Booksmitten* podcast crew, Kelly J. Baptist, Jack Cheng, and Heather Shumaker. And thanks to Jason Harper for the great weekend writing space.

Thanks to Michelle Duffy, Tami Mills, and Maria Scott for their subject expertise.

Thanks to Ernest Flores, King County librarians, and the late Peg Phillips for inviting me *inside* to meet locked-up teens.

Thanks for the eternal love and support of all the Scotts and Floreses. And thanks to Emma for choosing to walk side by side with me through every twist and turn of this oddball publishing path. Lastly, thanks to Carlos and Diego for believing in, and encouraging, their writer dad.

ABOUT THE AUTHOR

Patrick Flores-Scott is also the acclaimed author of the award-winning novels *Jumped In* and *American Road Trip*, which was named a YALSA Best Fiction Book, a TAYSHAS Reading List selection, an *SLJ* National Hispanic Heritage Month pick, and a *Teen Vogue* Best Gift Book and was licensed to WEBTOON for graphic digital serialization. Patrick taught public school in Seattle, Washington, for many years and has written for theater and the slam poetry stage. He lives in Ann Arbor, Michigan, with his family and invites you to visit him online at patrickfloresscott.com.